"You like me."

He pulled her to him. Dante didn't allow himself to consider defeat—he knew Ana was crazy about him. No woman made love to a man the way Ana did with him and honestly believed she wasn't in love with him.

No. Not just in love. She was crazy for him, just as much as he was for her.

It was the baby thing bugging her—he knew it had to be.

"Marry me."

He surprised both of them by saying it. But he felt great the moment he said it. Ana's eyes widened, and he thought, bingo, that was the right thing to say.

But then she shook her head, sending his world into dust. "I can't, Dante. You don't understand. I— It wouldn't work. We're not right for each other."

"You're exactly right for me."

Dear Reader,

In this eleventh book of the Callahan saga, we learn a lot about true love in the face of adventure—which is just what we want from our heroes and heroines! Summer is a wonderful time to dream about brave men and women fighting to do what's right, even if doing what's right isn't easy.

Dante Callahan, the first of the Chacon Callahan twins to suffer what he believes is unrequited love with the beautiful nanny bodyguard Ana St. John, sets out to prove himself on the bull-riding circuit. But he finds his place is back with the family…yet danger lurks. Dante never imagines that the way he'll finally get the bodyguard of his dreams in his arms is by allowing her to protect him—a difficult thing for a tough guy to accept! Ana St. John isn't about to give up on her man, however; she's been waiting a long while to find out if the rangy cowboy is the man of her dreams. According to the magic wedding dress, maybe he's *not*…if the Callahan legend is to be believed.

Yet we know there's always a happy ending at Rancho Diablo! And I hope you'll join me and the Callahans on this next book in the journey of the Callahan family toward happiness and true love.

Best wishes always,

Tina Leonard

Branded by a Callahan

TINA LEONARD

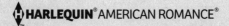
HARLEQUIN® AMERICAN ROMANCE®

Recycling programs
for this product may
not exist in your area.

ISBN-13: 978-0-373-75461-8

BRANDED BY A CALLAHAN

Copyright © 2013 by Tina Leonard

This edition published by arrangement with Harlequin Books S.A.

For questions and comments about the quality of this book,
please contact us at CustomerService@Harlequin.com.

® and TM are trademarks of Harlequin Enterprises Limited or its
corporate affiliates. Trademarks indicated with ® are registered in the
United States Patent and Trademark Office, the Canadian Trade Marks
Office and in other countries.

HARLEQUIN®
www.Harlequin.com

Printed in U.S.A.

ABOUT THE AUTHOR

Tina Leonard is a *USA TODAY* bestselling and award-winning author of more than fifty projects, including several popular miniseries for Harlequin American Romance. Known for bad-boy heroes and smart, adventurous heroines, her books have made the *USA TODAY*, Waldenbooks, Ingram and Nielsen BookScan bestseller lists. Born on a military base, Tina lived in many states before eventually marrying the boy who did her crayon printing for her in the first grade. You can visit her at www.tinaleonard.com, and follow her on Facebook and Twitter.

Books by Tina Leonard

HARLEQUIN AMERICAN ROMANCE

Many thanks to the wonderful readers who have taken the Callahans into their hearts

Chapter One

"If someone's looking for a fight with a Callahan, he'll sure find one."
—Bode Jenkins, neighboring ranch owner to a reporter asking questions about the Callahan legend

Dante Callahan stared at the enormous spotted bull pawing the ground and tossing its huge horns before climbing over the chute with a sense of impending doom. For his ride he'd drawn Firefreak, a bounty bull, and he'd started to wonder why he'd let his twin, Tighe, talk him into this. Dante had been working at the rodeo, practicing being a barrel man, doing a little mutton busting setup for the kiddies on the side, simply trying to keep Tighe out of trouble—though his twin seemed hell-bent on finding said trouble. Today his sole goal was to survive Firefreak, legendary badass rank bull. The last cowboy who'd ridden him—tried to ride him—had ended up in the hospital with broken bones.

All of this was to avoid Dante mooning over Ana St. John, the hot babe bodyguard who worked at Rancho Diablo.

Ana, who'd never glanced his way except by accident.

Dante got on the bull, settled himself with a choke hold on the rope, mashed his hat down on his head. Cowboys yelled encouragement, instructions, some various bits of garbled wisdom and maybe a prayer or two. He took a deep breath, nodded—and the chute burst open.

Hell hit Dante so fast he hung on by reflex. The jaw-grinding, butt-breaking bucking set his insides screaming, and then he was on the ground, staring up at nothing, before adrenaline shot him to his feet to scramble away from the pounding hooves intent on his destruction.

"That was awesome, bro!" Tighe yelled as Dante stumbled out of the arena. "Five seconds!"

Five seconds—of hell. Gasping, Dante held his heaving ribs, some of which ached like sin, and spit out his mouth guard. "My life passed before my eyes," he said, lurching to sit on a hay bale. "Holy smokes, I think I saw the face of God."

Tighe laughed, pounded him on the back. "You're fine. You're all right."

"Yeah. He didn't put me in the hospital."

Cowboys came by, shouting words at him he heard but that somehow didn't sink in. "I've got to do that again."

His twin handed him a water bottle. "On Firefreak?"

"Sorry piece of boot leather isn't going to defeat me." The thing was, for those glorious five seconds, it had been all about survival, sort of like when he'd been in Afghanistan, only more endurable because Firefreak was an enemy he had control of. Five seconds of nothing but a mind-numbing, desperate attempt to hang on—and he hadn't donated one of those seconds to thinking about Ana.

It had been glorious relief.

"We have enough points to move on," Tighe said. "Next rodeo, next ride."

Dante rubbed his rib, wiped his brow. "I'm going home, bro."

Tighe straightened, his expression shocked dismay. "Home to Rancho Diablo? Why?"

He couldn't explain it, not even to his twin. But Tighe must have felt it. The two of them practically shared every thought. "It's almost Halloween. I want to see the kids trick-or-treat." He sighed at the memory and felt strength washing over him. "There's nothing like seeing all the Callahan kinder dressed up like tiny ghosts and ballerinas."

Tighe smiled. "True."

"We've been gone for months, chasing this dream." He'd last gone home for a wedding in June, when his brother Falcon had married the light of his life, Taylor Waters. Feeling the call of the wild, Dante and Tighe had quit the family fold, leaving their brothers and sister to keep the enemy stalking Rancho Diablo at bay.

He'd worked out his wild oats. Or gotten them crushed out of him by the likes of Firefreak.

"You think you're over long-legged Ana of the streaming golden hair and luscious lips? I believe that's how you refer to her when you're thrashing in your sleep."

"Wasn't anything to get over." Dante wiped his face, brought away a little sawdust, sweat and a bit of blood. "I'm probably about as over her as you are over her buddy River. She of the teasing eyes and voice of a goddess, as you mumble after you've had a six-pack or so."

Tighe grunted. "Stay strong, bro. Denial is the first hint ye old heart still acheth."

"Shut up, Tighe." Maybe his twin was right, but the loyalty factor lately had reared its head in his thoughts. He could only ditch the family so long, wouldn't have ditched them at all if he hadn't felt a burning need to keep Tighe out of trouble. They'd almost never been separated, rarely even during their terms in Afghanistan. As SEALs, they weren't assigned to the same team, but they'd still been able to keep tabs on each other. "It's fine." He got up, happy that his body ached more than his heart. "It's more than fine."

"Good." Tighe stood beside him. "Don't think I have to tell you I'm not going."

"All in good time." Dante shrugged. "It's whatever."

"You gonna marry her?"

Dante laughed. "I'm not a marrying man."

"You act like a marrying man, all soreheaded whenever anyone mentions Ana."

"I don't want to marry her." The nanny bodyguard, who protected Sloan and Kendall's little boys from potential kidnappers, was smooth and tall, and when she walked it was more of a stalk, like a sexy panther. His throat tended to dry out just watching Ana move, as if he was a dog watching a bone swing just out of reach. His heart kicked into overdrive and his, well… Suffice it to say he had a burn that wouldn't quit around her. Sometimes he was positive Ana had been brought to the ranch just to torture him with sweet, restless dreams; his own hell for longing for beauty and goodness in his life these days, punishment exacted for the sins he'd committed. "I think I want to sleep with her. Surely that's all it is."

"Maybe, maybe not." Tighe shook his head. "Sometimes one thing leads to another."

"Doubt it."

"Why don't you just spend the night with her then and quit going around like someone's shot you full of holes?"

"Because I'm afraid of her." Dante took off some of his gear. Making up his mind felt great. He'd faced the worst of what a rank bull had to offer, now he could face the rest of what he needed to. "She's so radioactive that I'm afraid I'd never get over it once I—"

"That's fine." Tighe shuddered. "There's nothing more devastating than lust when emotion is involved. It's good old-fashioned sex with no strings for me, or I'm not getting near it."

"Yeah, well, cry me a river." Dante packed up his stuff. "Good luck at the next ride."

"You're leaving today?" Tighe's brows went sky-high. Disappointment was etched in his navy eyes, and Dante felt another stab of disloyalty for leaving his twin behind.

"Gotta be home in time for tricks or treats." It really was something to behold, seeing almost two dozen Callahan children running around munching on popcorn balls and candy corn. Ghost stories would be told— gently—and hot apple cider drunk. He wasn't about to miss the fun. There'd be pony rides and a ghost piñata for the tiniest to swing at with a sponge bat. "I'm heading for Hell's Colony first for tricks-'n-treats, then on to Rancho Diablo for the real haunting."

Tighe smirked. "You'll be back with me on the circuit soon. I give it two, three weeks. As soon as you realize you'd rather be riding Firefreak than being invisible to the nanny bodyguard goddess, you'll hotfoot it right back. You know where to find me."

"Yeah. Happy trails. Don't bust your noggin. See ya, bro." He grabbed his stuff and headed off, looking forward to testing himself against the ultimate green-eyed fire.

THE HUGE SPREAD in Hell's COLONY, Texas, was a compound, actually, owned by the Phillips family. Beautiful Kendall Phillips had married his brother Sloan, and when the Callahans had needed a place to hide out for a while, Kendall had offered her family home. It had turned out nicely for all because it kept all the Diablo Callahans together, and safe from those that meant them harm.

The Callahan children loved being together. Halloween night was no exception, and almost two dozen diminutive ghosts, tiny pumpkins, some petite pea pods still in carriers and a few larger Cinderellas and Zorros ran around holding pillowcases for the treats they hoped to collect. Moms were dressed as anything from Raggedy Ann to Glinda the Good Witch from Oz, and Dante laughed at some of his cousins and their getups. He was feeling pretty good about his own costume— a black mask, black cowboy hat and jingling spurs. He was channeling "cowboy rascal"—maybe the outfit wasn't far off enough to be a costume—when Ana slinked past him wearing what could only be termed as a nurse's uniform, and suddenly Dante lacked the serenity he'd previously boasted of to his twin. Oh, he guessed it wasn't a sexy costume in the classical sense; she didn't wear garters, and there were none of the frills that went along with the tacky version of the nurse's uniform. She was simply dressed in purple scrubs. Purple top, purple pants, long hair up in a streaming gold ponytail, and high tan cork sandals. It wasn't supposed to be sexy. She was, after all, a nanny—or bodyguard, take your pick—to Sloan's twins, but as far as Dante was concerned, Ana could wear a plastic trash sack and his adrenaline would still jet into overdrive.

Tighe had been so right.

Blast.

"Hi, Dante," Ana said, and he gulped.

"Hi, Ana." He wanted to tell her how beautiful she looked, but he didn't want to sound like a thickheaded sad sack, which his brothers would tell him he was. So he swallowed his real thoughts back.

"Long time, no see." She beamed at him as if he was a man among men, and he grew uncomfortably hot under his black mask. "How's the rodeo?"

"Good enough." He was tongue-tied, which only happened around *her.*

"I'm off to take the children through the haunted house. It's really a couple of rooms in one of the guesthouses we set up with Clifford the Big Red Dog story time and a Candyland trail. Joining us later?"

Emerald eyes blinked at him sweetly. He could think of nothing he'd like more than to join her in a haunted house, or any house at all. "Sure."

She gave him a last big smile and stalked off, pantherlike and graceful, and Dante knew he was doomed. Tighe could probably pick up his heated brain waves from seven hundred miles away and was doubled over laughing, not to mention counting off the three weeks he expected his twin to last under the onslaught of blinding lust Dante experienced around Ana.

"Have you been putting a little adult additive into the cider, bro?" Ash asked, looking up at him, concerned. "Your eyes are all glazed over."

"I wish. Got any?"

His sister giggled. "Nope. Around the kiddies we abstain. After they go to bed, though, I heard Fiona's got special libations for us. Black martinis and bloody rum punch, if I heard her right. We all only get one, so you better hustle to claim yours if you want to enjoy the paranormal experience. You've been assigned to the sponge piñata event. I've got to go shepherd pitching pennies into pumpkins." His sister went off, throwing herself into the kiddie fray with enthusiasm.

It was so good to be home. Dante went to run the sponge piñata, pretty certain he needed more than a howling-good drink if he was going to survive staring at Ana with no kisses planned for him on her Hallows Eve schedule.

AFTER THE MUNCHKIN MAYHEM, the evening was quiet. The adults sat around the kitchen, satisfied that the children had gone to bed with visions of candy corn and Clifford the Big Red Dog dancing in their heads. Dante sucked at his black martini, happy he hadn't missed the mayhem. It really was the best part of being in a large family, which he was, now that his clan had found the long lost Callahans of his missing father's brother, Jeremiah.

He and his six siblings were helping their Callahan cousins until the evil had passed from their home in New Mexico. The cousins stayed here in Hell's Colony with the wives and children, and Dante and his siblings tried to stay one step ahead of trouble at Rancho Diablo. Basically bodyguards for hire, assigned by the head of the Callahan clan, Chief Running Bear.

It wasn't always easy. So far on their watch, three kidnappings had taken place—two of the women and one brother, Falcon. He and his six siblings were military operatives, raised in the tribe and tough to sneak up on—yet despite their best efforts, they'd found themselves under attack, too.

When Tighe had taken off to rodeo, Dante had joined him, though he'd felt like a traitor to his Callahan cousins, his brothers and sister and Aunt Fiona by leaving.

Ashlyn plopped down next to him, a pile of candy corns in a bowl her offering to him. "Cheer up. The kiddies didn't beat you with the sponge bat. The ghost piñata was popped, and candy dispensed. Good times, good times."

He grinned at his silver-blond-haired sister who was dressed like a sparkling fairy sprite. "How come you got to go off post tonight? Thought all the operatives were staying at Rancho Diablo to be on the safe side."

"Because I'm fun. We flipped for it, and Jace, Galen and Falcon came up short. Sloan got to come for the fun because his twins are almost old enough to know what's going on. They were darling little pea pods." She grinned. "That's why Ana and River are here."

He glanced at the nanny bodyguards as surreptitiously as possible, caught Ana sneaking a peek at him. He remembered he was still wearing his black mask and removed it, figuring he didn't need the Lone Ranger vibe anymore.

"I missed you, you know, even if you're a schmuck," Ash said cheerfully. "Staying awhile this time?"

"I'm back for good."

"You won't run away from your heart again?"

He sighed, sipping the martini, thinking it wasn't any blacker than his hopes at the moment. "I'm in for the long haul."

"Good." She looked satisfied. "Shall we make a wager?"

"If we must."

"I wager you'll figure out a way to romance Ana by Christmas." She grinned. "Sloan and Falcon fell much more easily than I ever dreamed. You should be a piece of cake. You're a softie and already have your target in sight."

He'd already fallen, so the wager was lopsided. Ana had never given him the time of day, no more than River gave Tighe any reason to hope. Only Jace seemed to hold the key to the bodyguards, and that alone was annoying. "Trust me, I'd be more than willing to wager whatever you wanted, if I thought there was half a chance. I don't wager when the house deck is stacked against me."

"It's for charity," Ash said. "I'm trying to raise five hundred bucks for the horse rescue in Diablo. Pony up, bro. If you win—which would actually be losing, but never mind—I'll give you your money back." Her face held nothing but purposeful honesty. "You can trust me."

"Okay." He reached into his wallet, tossed out his rodeo winnings.

She beamed. "Money well spent. Just putting your money where your dreams are is practically a guarantee of good things happening for you!"

His sister went off, delighted that she'd lightened him of all he had on him at the moment. Dante sipped his drink again, catching Ana's gaze on him before she hurriedly looked at her punch.

Well, it wasn't the mask, he'd removed that. He hadn't shaved, but women didn't usually get real excited over scruffy cheeks, so that probably wasn't what had her peeking. His hair was far too long—he hadn't seen a barber in months—and so maybe he did look a bit wild. His nieces and nephews had lavished him with attention, a returning hero in their eyes, so at least he wasn't completely Grizzly Adams–wild-looking if he didn't scare small children.

Ana came over and sat next to him, and Dante was so shocked he nearly swallowed the floating olive eyeball in his drink.

"Happy Halloween," she said, and he felt a tickle of something slide up his spine. Ah, yes, sexual attraction, the bane of his useless designs on Ana.

"Same to you."

His tongue twisted up like the lemon garnish on her drink.

"Your sister says you're the resident ghost-storyteller."

Generous of Ash to throw him an opener for conversation with Ana. "I'm afraid I enjoyed frightening my sister and brothers whether it was Halloween or not."

She smiled. He was lost in her eyes and that sexy smile. "I love ghost stories."

He was getting a funny feeling that something was going on here. Ana seemed to be chatting him up—and it could all be just friendly, but then again, maybe—

Nah. She hadn't spoken to him in anything more than a professional tone for all the months he'd lived at Rancho Diablo. "What's on your mind, cupcake?"

She looked at him. "Cupcake?"

He had to hide behind alpha-male bravado to save his sanity. His wisdom had been too hard-won over the past several months—and the tearing that Firefreak had given him was a reminder not to make a fool of himself again on useless pining. "I just thought maybe you had something on your mind."

"I do," Ana said, and Dante blinked.

"Oh?" If she, too, had a horse charity, his pockets were as empty as old boots.

"I have the evening off," Ana said, "and I was wondering if you'd like to—"

The doorbell rang, gonging throughout the palatial house. Everyone glanced at Kendall, since it was her family home. "I gave the butler the night off, and he went into town," Kendall said.

Dante glanced at his sister. Ash's brows rose. There hadn't been any trick-or-treaters. No one could get past the gated entrance.

Kendall had a sniper on the roof to keep an eye on Jonas Callahan's clan, make certain none of the mercenaries got close to any of the children or wives.

The mercs had tried for years to find the Callahan parents, but so far, it was Callahans riding to the buzzer, and the mercenaries—including their black sheep, evil uncle Wolf—unable to get anything going.

Dante got up. "I'll go to the door."

Everyone looked at him. Ana got up, too. "I'll play backup."

He didn't need backup from a woman, even if she was a bodyguard with great references from several high-profile clients. His sister was the only woman who'd ever "backed" him up. He glanced at Ashlyn who grinned hugely and had the nerve to wave the stash of loot of which she'd stripped him.

But he couldn't turn Ana down—it would be rude and decidedly un-Callahan. Dante went off down the long hall to the front door with Ana behind him. When he opened the huge wooden door, he was somehow not at all surprised to find a gun pointed at his face.

"Trick or treat," the masked cowboy said. "Step outside and close the door."

Nuts. Dante walked out, prepared to protect Ana at all costs, when she slipped around him and sprayed something in the cowboy's face. He howled and pawed at his eyes, and Ana took the opportunity to kick his legs out from underneath him and tie his wrists behind his back like a cowgirl tying off a roped calf.

"There," Ana said, standing up, "he's all yours."

The man on the ground cursed, swearing about the burning in his eyes and how much he hated the Callahans in general. Dante grinned at his beautiful "backup" wearing purple scrubs and a sexy smile, his heart thundering like the mystical Diablo mustangs in the Rancho Diablo canyons, and thought, *You're all mine, gorgeous.*

You just don't know it yet.

Chapter Two

Two hours later, the intruder had been trundled off by the local sheriff, and the sniper who'd been on duty was located—shot with a tranquilizer dart.

All the Callahans were grouped into the big white formal room that Kendall had always claimed she hated until the Callahans had taken over her compound. Now toy trucks and baby dolls lay in neat baskets lining a wall, and another basket of crayons and coloring books lay stacked near the ebony grand piano. An overly industrious child—he thought it might have been one of Pete's triplets—had done a little Picasso-style artwork on the wall near the floorboard, in what looked very much like sky-blue and magenta, two colors he remembered well from his own days of coloring.

"This is bad," Dante told his cousins, brothers and sister. Jonas nodded, as did the others. No one had told Aunt Fiona or Uncle Burke—yet. They'd have to be informed of this new development. They'd gone to bed after the Halloween festivities, and Dante saw no reason to rouse them when there was nothing they could do now. "What if Aunt Fiona had opened the door?"

Ana met his gaze. He thought he could sense her concern, which matched his.

"Fiona *would* have opened the door, if she'd been in the family room or kitchen," Sloan said. "But someone meant business if they took out the sniper and then presented themselves on the front porch as a trick-or-treater."

Ash shivered. "Lucky for you Ana went to the door with you, Dante."

Dante frowned. "I can take care of myself, thanks."

He was a highly trained SEAL. He didn't need Ana—or anyone else—to take care of him.

Though it had been rather glorious to watch those curves in motion as she'd taken down the thug. Just remembering it brought a smile to his face.

"What's so funny?" Ash demanded, staring at him. "You could have been killed."

Dante shook his head. "I'm like a cat, and I've only used up about seven of my nine lives. No one's gonna take me out."

Ana's eyes were huge. Okay, so maybe things could have gotten a little dicey if she hadn't put her training and quick wits to use. "Let's just focus on the plan going forward. The first thing we need to discuss is security. Obviously, the Phillips' compound has been breached. We've inadvertently brought the fight here."

They all considered that. "I think it's pretty safe," Ash said. "It's taken them a long time to try an attack here."

"They're watching the ranch," Ana said suddenly. "They knew half of us would be here in Hell's Colony. Has anybody checked on the guys back at Rancho Diablo?"

Dante looked at Ana, considered her words, felt himself falling just a little bit more for a woman whose mind worked so quickly and looked so stunning doing it. It was as if a Greek warrior goddess had come to life, tempting him to kiss her.

He was going to have to do that real soon. "Ash, send a text to Galen, Falcon and Jace. See if you get a response."

"On it," she said, grabbing her phone.

"The sheriff didn't have any idea who he was," Ana said, "which means he's from outside Hell's Colony. He had no ID on him. That's deliberate."

"Yeah," Dante agreed. "A Halloween ambush. It's just all too convenient."

"I think so, too," Ana said. "There's no way the man on the porch is the one who shot the sniper with the tranquilizer."

Dante looked at her. "Why not? I took out plenty of armed—"

Ash cleared her throat. "Oh," Dante said, "right." It was a Halloween party, after all, no need to bring up past assignments, especially since the darling nanny bodyguard had defended him. He'd feel deflated about that except Ana was just so darn hot. Maybe he was weird or what his brothers would call judiciously individual, but Ana defending him gave him a superbad case of heat he didn't think he was going to recover from anytime soon. "Okay, Ana, are you working on a theory?"

She nodded. "I think our Halloween visitor has a companion out there."

Ash sat up. "Waiting."

"That's right." Ana nodded, and Dante watched her, considering her suddenly very plausible idea. "The guy on the porch was just the sideshow. The distraction."

Dante's blood went cold. "Has anybody checked on Fiona and Burke?"

Ash's eyes went huge, and then she tore up the stairs. Dante could feel his heart beating hard in his chest until his sister returned.

"Out like lights," Ash reported. "And I don't think Fiona holds herself and Burke to the one-martini rule." She sniffed. "There's a crystal pitcher of bloody rum punch by their bed. And a plate of her delicious gingerbread ghosts, but we won't hold that against her."

Ana sat thinking quietly. "What?" Dante demanded. "I can tell you're working on something."

"It just doesn't add up. He barely put up a fight."

"He didn't have a chance," Dante told her. "You were on him too quickly. He didn't know what hit him."

"No." She shook her head. "He didn't put up much resistance at all."

"You gave him a faceful of pepper spray," Ash pointed out. "That might wear down my resistance a bit."

Ana got up, pacing a bit, which Dante appreciated because he loved watching her move. It was a ballet on cork sandals, body parts moving sexily, gracefully.

"Someone was with him. Someone took out the sniper, then played lookout. We called the sheriff, and two hours later he's in a cell." Ana shook her head. "Have you heard back from Rancho Diablo?" she asked Ashlyn.

"All present and accounted for," Ash said.

"This is all so suspicious," Ana said, sitting down next to Dante. His blood pressure went to the roof of his skull, drumming loudly. He smelled sweet perfume and warm woman, and it was everything he could do not to reach out and take her hand in his.

She'd be so shocked if he did.

"If we don't think anyone could have breached the house, then it's something else," Ana said.

It suddenly hit Dante that Ana was working from a hunch. As a guy who'd relied upon his hunches at times to stay alive, Dante found himself paying close attention to what Ana was trying to tease through. "What else is likely?" he asked.

She finally glanced at him. "I don't know."

He nodded. "We'll know soon enough."

"The thing is," Ana said, staring earnestly into his eyes, "it feels too coincidental. It feels too easy. Career mercenaries don't make mistakes. That's why I think it was a cover for something else."

"Maybe just to keep us on edge?" Ash asked.

"I don't think so." Ana shook her head. "I'll go to bed and think about it. Maybe it will come to me in the night."

"Sounds like a good idea." Dante stood, began stacking the glasses on a tray. Halloween had come and gone for another year. Thanksgiving would arrive next, always a family gathering of great camaraderie and joy—and then Christmas. But the costumes and carved pumpkins would disappear for another year, which made him a bit nostalgic.

Why pick Halloween for an ambush?

He and Ana carried the small dishes and glasses to the kitchen. "Have you talked to Tighe today?"

He shook his head. He didn't want to think about his loony brother at this moment. "I haven't heard much from him. He's been busy getting brained by bulls."

She nodded. "Okay. Good night."

He stared after her as she passed into the hallway. He heard her sandals on the marble floor.

"Drooling is only cute when babies do it," Ashlyn told him, giving him a nudge. "Need a bib?"

He probably was drooling. Turning back to the dishes, he put them in the dishwasher. "Not sure there's a bib big enough."

His sister looked up at him. "You know, you can treat Ana like she's a normal girl, not some kind of princess you have to put in an ivory tower. I have it on good authority that she doesn't bite."

"She might." Dante didn't care how much his sister ribbed him about Ana—he might be slow in his windup, but eventually, he'd work his way into the game. "Don't think it's escaped my attention that you, little sister, are working on quite the unrequited thing for one of the owners of this compound, and everybody's favorite canyon-riding cowboy, Xav Phillips."

Ash glared at him. "Am I supposed to say ouch?" She tossed her head. "At least I would kiss Xav if he got close enough. Ana saved you. The least you can do is put down the barbed wire fence."

He grunted, wondered about Tighe. Why had Ana asked about his twin?

"The kids love her," Ash said, washing out some glasses. "I bet Ana will make a wonderful mother."

He blinked. "Is she going to be a mother?"

"Maybe."

Ash didn't clarify, and he wasn't about to give her anything else to rib him about by asking. He had to go with the flow around here, especially where Ana was concerned, or he'd end up a laughingstock.

Ash sighed. "Did you at least thank her for saving you?"

"No."

"Then I'll thank her for saving my big brother,"

Ash said. "I appreciate what she did. If people aren't acknowledged when they do a good job, sometimes they find another employer."

He got the hint and decided not to encourage his sister. "I'll let you finish up here."

His sister snapped his butt with a dish towel as he departed. "Good night, dear brother."

He went out to the guest quarters, which consisted of three bedrooms and a small kitchenette. This is where he was bunking—and tonight, the sniper was also taking up one of the rooms, sleeping off the effects of the tranquilizer, which the doctor said wouldn't last forever. They hadn't gotten much out of the man because he mostly wanted to snooze, but one thing was clear: he didn't want to go to a hospital. Said he'd be fine sleeping outside. They'd stuck him out here with Dante, who was fine with checking on him occasionally.

Thing was, without the sniper on the roof of the compound, they were pretty much without cover. Someone had known the sniper was there—and had taken him out with enough tranquilizer to give an elephant a bit of a Rip van Winkler. Dante went into his room, his thoughts in a snarl, trying to make sense of the whole thing—but his brain stopped cold when he flipped on the light and saw the gorgeous blonde in his bed. Sound asleep, looking like an angel.

Holy smokes, what was he supposed to do with this?

He turned the overhead light off. Pondered his next move. Clearly Ana hadn't wanted to sleep in the main house. Did she have the night off? He supposed she must have. After one black martini with a floating eyeball in it, was he relaxed enough to take advantage of the heavenly gift in his bed?

Absolutely not.

Dante felt like he was sneaking around in his own room. Maybe she'd been scared, and didn't want to be alone.

Nah. Ana hadn't been the least bit intimidated.

Maybe he should just turn around, walk back through the door, forget what he'd seen. Pretend he'd felt better sleeping in the main house tonight—

The lamp beside the bed turned on, and Dante's throat went dry as an old bone in the desert. Ana looked at him, her gaze curious.

"Hi, cowboy."

Long blond hair draped silkily over one shoulder. She hadn't changed out of her purple scrubs, but the cork sandals lay on the floor beside her.

Okay, gifts this good didn't just drop into his life. There was a trap, he just couldn't see it. His concentration was shot, and any warning system he'd ever possessed that normally blared caution in a danger zone had surrendered. "Howdy, nurse," he finally said, trying to play it cool. "I do believe you're in the wrong bed."

"Maybe," Ana said. "But I hope not."

He couldn't mistake the soft invitation, nor the smoke in those emerald eyes. The lady was offering, and all he had to do was get rid of the barbed wire fence Ash claimed he was hiding behind. "All right," he said, his voice husky, his throat a bit stiff for some reason. "You tell me what you want, lady, and I'll see if I can accommodate you."

Safe enough. Let her state her mission—maybe she was only scared, after all—and he'd see if he could help her out.

She turned out the lamp. He heard sheets rustle, and the next thing he knew she was moving into his arms. Her lips found his, and it was everything Dante had ever imagined kissing Ana would be like: soft, sweet, powerful.

He didn't ask any questions. He hung on like he'd hung on to Firefreak, praying he didn't hit the ground too soon.

"I'm going to get a little more comfortable," she said, moving out of his arms, "maybe you will, too."

She went into the bathroom, closed the door behind her. His heart thundered like mad, a haze practically shutting down his brain. After all the months of longing, he was going to find himself holding the most beautiful woman in the world.

He pulled off his boots, kept his jeans and shirt on just in case the invitation got jerked away from him at the last minute. Waited in the dark, his body taut with anticipation.

The bathroom door opened, and he heard soft footsteps approach the bed. It was too dark for him to get the full effect, but maybe she was shy about him seeing her in the dark. Wouldn't matter. He'd run his lips over every inch of that long, slinky body, and he'd have no problem whatsoever seeing everything he wanted to with his hands.

Something soft brushed his face, molded over his nose and mouth with a strange scent—but by then it was too late for Dante to react, even as his last thought was that the world's most beautiful angel had just played him like the queen of hearts.

Chapter Three

Bumps and jolts jarred Dante painfully awake. Opening his eyes, he stared at a dark sky overhead, felt the cold of a truck bed beneath him as it trundled over ruts on what was obviously a country road. His hands and ankles seemed bound together—make that *were* bound. His boots lay near his head, confirming that he'd been hijacked.

Last night's sudden and sweet seduction had been nothing but a sham. Ana St. John was a spy, a double-crosser in the first degree. He could see it all clearly now: she'd been working with whoever had taken out the sniper, and she'd followed Dante to the front door to pretend to save him Halloween night, throwing off suspicion.

All the while she'd been planning his downfall with a body made to stun. Like Samson cut down by Delilah, Dante had allowed Ana to blind him to common sense.

Love did indeed stink to high heaven.

A particularly vicious rut sent him bouncing skyward, and something moaned—not him. Glancing across the truck bed, he saw Ana in pretty much the same condition as he, only she had on less clothes to keep out the November chill. She, too, was bound, still wearing her scrubs, though the cork sandals didn't appear to have made the trip.

Dante was cheered by her presence, but he also felt like a louse. Being happy when one's object of desire was trussed up like a chicken, obviously being kidnapped along with him, was the mark of a truly pathetically gone heart.

He was so relieved Ana hadn't played him. He would have felt like a bigger putz than all his brothers combined.

Ana opened her eyes, glanced around in rather shocked fashion, as he had, then saw him smiling at her. "Fancy meeting you here, cupcake."

She blinked, looked annoyed. "This was not supposed to happen!"

"Yeah, well. Just an adventure to tell the grandkids, I guess." He kept his tone soothing and light so she wouldn't panic. Females were so delicate, and it was his job to comfort the gentler species, especially this darling one. He frowned. "Wait, what wasn't supposed to happen?"

"I've never been jumped." Ana glanced around the truck bed. "No one has ever been able to catch me off guard, and that's a record I was extremely proud of. Who took us?"

"We'll know soon enough."

"Where are we?"

"My guess? Far from home. The air's got a trace of petroleum. Definitely a chemical. I'm guessing somewhere around Houston."

"Or Louisiana."

It would stand to reason. They'd clearly been on the road a long time because his body was screaming from all the jags and bumps. He needed to hit a rest stop in the worst way. "They must have grabbed you in the lavatory, because I never saw you come out. And I would definitely have remembered."

"First bad mark on my record." Pure annoyance crossed her face. "I didn't check the bath when I snuck in, and I should have."

"Rule number one in the bodyguard manual broken," he said cheerfully. "I won't tell if you don't." He didn't care, because she freely admitted sneaking into his room, and from that, he could deduce that this beautiful woman dug her some Callahan cowboy.

"I failed to protect you," Ana said.

"Oh, I won't hold it against you," Dante said, thinking he was fine with role reversal. He was the man, he was supposed to be doing the protecting, and moreover, they'd only grabbed her because of him—she was a collateral situation. None of this would be happening right now if he weren't a Callahan, which left very little blame to be parked at her door. "Anyway, I'm the man, I'm supposed to protect the fairer sex."

"Are we going to debate sexual roles or figure out how to get out of this mess?"

He liked the idea of debating sexual anything with Ana, but he supposed her question was relevant. But then he had a horrible thought: his grandfather, Chief Running Bear, had muttered something about one of the seven Chacon Callahans being the hunted one. Running Bear had intoned the warning with such fierce knowledge, and Dante had always figured it couldn't possibly be him.

But what if he *was* the one of which Running Bear warned? Any last vestige of grogginess from whatever they'd used to dope him disappeared, and his focus returned, laserlike.

"What?" Ana said. "You look like you want to kill something."

He wasn't going to worry about it now. If he was the hunted one, he'd get unhunted fast. Darkness had fallen, blanketing the truck's path. His body felt like a yo-yo from the pounding bumps in the road, and Ana couldn't be in any better shape. "We've got to get out of here."

"Following you, cowboy."

She was a sparky little thing, he'd grant her that. "For what it's worth, I appreciated finding you in my bed. Hope you don't let this experience scare you from trying again."

Ana gave him a wry look. "Not at all," she said sweetly. "I've picked you to be the father of my child."

A hard jolt sent them both rolling, and covered the yelp Dante might have let go upon hearing Ana's pronouncement. "You meant it wasn't just about my body?"

"No." Ana rolled close to him, which he thought was very sweet of her, very sexy. He liked women who were so pointed about their desire. "Undo my hands, please," Ana told him.

"Ah." Romance would have to wait; this little doll was all about business. He backed up to her, grabbed her bound hand with his and worked off the knotted handkerchief. "Free as a bird."

Without creating any movement that would alert their kidnappers, she untied her feet. "Blast, they didn't bring my shoes. That's men for you. They never consider the important stuff."

"They brought my boots," Dante said, a bit relieved by that. He could carry Ana on his back if he had to.

"I may borrow those boots, cowboy."

He looked at her. "Oh, no, you don't, cupcake. If you think for one second that you're going to take my boots and leave me stranded here with a couple of jokers, you will never get what you came for last night."

She reached for a boot, looked him in the eye. "You may not be able to give me a child. It's a calculated risk."

There was absolutely nothing he'd rather do than give impregnating this sweet angel the old college try. "I offer my family tree as Exhibit A. You're the nanny, you should know that Callahans are prodigious baby makers."

She considered that. "True. Yet I find it highly suspicious that you're not running. Men are supposed to run when a woman tells them they want a child."

"Yeah, but I'm not a normal guy."

"This, I've heard."

She undid his hands, which he'd expected, since it was obvious she did indeed want to test his pregnancy prowess. He smirked, trying to look like a man who had full confidence that a baby bingo was as easy as snapping the fingers. "What's the big hurry on getting pregnant? You have a biological clock going off?"

Ana barely gave him a glance. "You focus on the mission, which is saving us. Let me worry about my reasons." She hesitated. "How do I know you'll keep your promise?"

He kissed her briefly, just a soft brush of promised pleasure against her lips. "Because, beautiful, I guarantee satisfaction."

She finished undoing him and his hands came free.

He grabbed her, pulling her lips to his, cradling her head in his hands so that he could kiss her as thoroughly as he'd ever wanted to. "Consider that a down payment."

"I do. I promise to make your life miserable if you try to back out of our deal. Remember, I could have taken your boots and left you here."

"I'd hate for you to live with those regrets. One day you'll thank your lucky stars I kept you, despite the fact that you'll be a drag on the mission." He pulled on his boots, watching her. She was a spicy girl for sure, and one day, he was going to dive in and enjoy the fire. "Now hang on, this is where it gets rough, gorgeous."

He wrapped his arms around her, held her tight.

"What are you doing?"

"Watch and learn. Focus," he whispered in her ear. "The truck has slowed. We're no longer on the main road, we're obviously getting closer to the destination. They've slowed, looking for a meeting point. The road isn't hard and rocky anymore, feels more like sand. Perfect."

"Perfect for what?"

"Finding out what little girls are made of. I always heard it was sugar and spice, but let's hope you're more spice than sugar."

He flipped her over the edge of the truck, still holding her tight. They landed with a thud in a not-so-soft patch of dried sand liberally laced with grit. To Ana's credit she didn't make a peep, and Dante held his breath, praying that the truck kept on its slow way to its destination.

It did. "Let's go. We have about five minutes, maybe less, before they discover we flew the coop."

"Head away from the road," Ana said, and Dante

thought, *Yeah, I had a feeling she was spice,* and they ran until they crossed a smaller road that was more of a dirt-bike path.

They stopped, and Dante plotted his bearings. "Due north," he said, pointing. "Heading to the west gets us back home."

"How do you know they didn't take us west?"

"I was watching the sky. The North star always guides us."

"I must have missed that lesson." Ana took off her shirt, tore it in half, bound up her feet for protection. "What are you staring at? It's a sports bra."

He was staring because being this close to heaven might just kill him. Sports bra or not, she was a tantalizing twist and slope of delicate curves and just-right softness. Tiny little waist. Athletic body. He swallowed, tore his eyes away with effort. A huge effort.

Dante cleared his throat even though it felt as if it was suddenly made of industrial rubber. "You ran pretty dang fast for a girl who was barefoot. I'm sorry." There'd probably been burrs or sticker grass in the sand loam road.

"Sorry for what?" Ana glared at him. "I can take care of myself. I can take care of you, too."

He smiled. "You are the most precious little thing I've ever come across."

"And you may be the biggest donkey I've ever laid eyes on." Her glare deepened. "Has it ever occurred to you that not every female is just waiting for you to bring your big muscles and your annoying chauvinism to rescue her?"

A grin split his face. "You like my big muscles?"

"Yes, I do. Can we discuss your manliness another time?"

"It's never a bad time to discuss that," Dante said, and they began walking toward the west, staying well out of sight of the main road. "Because I was thinking," Dante said, "if you like the muscles you can see, I've got some others that may—"

"Save it for later," Ana said. "I don't want you to blow a fuse."

"Pretty sure my fuses are fine." He was enormously pleased with the turn of events. Ana was awesome, just like he'd always suspected, and the best part was that the woman of his dreams wanted to have his baby.

It couldn't be denied that he was catnip to the sweet thing. "I'm going to take good care of you, Ana."

"Keep talking, and you'll probably find yourself in trouble," she said sweetly, and he said, "I like trouble. Trouble is a good friend of mine," before taking her hand in his as they hurried to make their escape.

THEY FOUND A SMALL, run-down motel in a one-horse town that didn't look as if it ever had much traffic. They were still in Texas, but hundreds of miles east of Hell's Colony. The owner was friendly and offered them breakfast in the morning if they were willing to get up early. "I like to start my knitting at eight, and once I start, I don't like to stop," she said with a genuinely friendly smile. "If I'm on my quilting, I definitely don't quit."

Ana looked at Dante, figuring he'd go for the breakfast over sleep. He shrugged at her, so she said, "I think we'll be gone by eight, Mrs. Adams. But thank you."

"I'll put together a couple of sack breakfasts, then." She waved them to a room upstairs and told them to sleep comfortably and not to mind any rattling they might hear. "It's just the air conditioner," she said helpfully, and Ana closed their bedroom door with a little relief.

"I thought she was going to say she had a ghost," Ana said. "These small towns always have a ghost, don't they?"

She pulled off the new moccasins Dante had bought her in a small outpost trading store. They were soft and comfortable, but they weren't as cute as her cork sandals.

"What have you got against ghosts?" Dante asked, lounging on the bed, hands behind his head. "Rancho Diablo's got ghosts."

"So I hear." She didn't believe it. Every once in a while Fiona got wound up about the ghosts and spirits that hung around the ranch, and Ana just listened to the tales, not about to give credence to one thing Fiona said. "I'm going to shower."

"Ladies first." He grinned, a sexy devil, and Ana wondered why he didn't seem more concerned about the fact that she had her eyes on him for a baby.

"While I'm in here, you can ask that nice Mrs. Adams if you could use the phone," she suggested.

"For what?"

"To call home, E.T." She sighed. "Dante, we don't want to walk all the way back to Hell's Colony."

"Oh. That." He shrugged. "I've got my mobile in my pocket."

She blinked. "Is there a reason we've been walking for miles and you haven't called for a pickup?"

"I like your company, sugar."

He was so aggravating that Ana wondered for a split second if she'd chosen the right man to give her a child.

Lord, yes. She had no second thoughts about that. She'd waited over a year to cross her professional boundaries and finally succumb to the die-hard attraction she had for this man. "I like yours, too, Dante," she said, trying to hang on to her temper. "But I think we'd like each other's company so much better if we weren't running from goons."

"Safer this way." He shrugged. "We'll wait another day before we call. I've got my mobile when we're ready, got my wallet, got you, doll." He grinned. "What else does a man need?"

"Okay." She went into the bathroom, turned on the shower. Callahans were known to be wired differently, so she couldn't say she was surprised that he'd choose walking across the state of Texas in dirty clothes preferable to calling for family pickup. She opened the door again. "Do you think you ought to let your family know we're fine?"

"They know. I texted them immediately once you untied my hands." He grinned, the biggest rascal on the planet. "You didn't notice because you were trying to protect me from our kidnappers as we walked. I just let you think you were doing all the work, angel."

She closed the bathroom door with a bit of force. "The apple didn't fall far from his brother apples," she muttered, stripping down.

A knock on the door made her jerk a towel to cover herself. "Yes?"

"Just wondering if I should scope out the bathroom for you this time."

She glanced around the tiny bath. "Think I've got it under control."

"Good to hear. If you don't mind, if you won't be nervous being left, I think I'm going to go scare us up some food."

Why had he mentioned her being afraid? She was

a bodyguard, her job was to protect, and technically, she was protecting Callahans, under which labeling he could be claimed. But he seemed to think she was just a girl, an ornament, and probably figured her main worth was cooking and cleaning.

He'd be really surprised when he learned that she couldn't cook and didn't clean a bit. She was a girl who worked, and she hadn't gone to bodyguard training to jump when a big lug like him snapped his chauvinistic fingers at her.

"I'm fine," she said, somewhat curious that he hadn't bothered to slip into the shower with her with some dumb excuse about conserving water for the diligent, quilting Mrs. Adams.

"Be right back."

There was silence after that. Ana enjoyed a long hot shower, and even considered taking a bath and soaking her feet. After several hours of walking, through some terrain one couldn't exactly call smooth because Dante was determined that they stay hidden from main roads where they might be seen—her feet weren't exactly thrilled with the treatment they'd endured.

They'd be home soon enough. She'd go for a manicure and pedicure with River, indulge in some girly maintenance, the kind meant to lure her cowboy into bed since he didn't seem all that inclined to get there real fast on his own.

Maybe he was more worried about the baby-making scheme than he'd let on.

A knock sounded on the door.

"Ana?"

"Yes?" She hesitated, wondering if he wanted—finally!—in the shower with her.

"Just letting you know I'm back."

Ana thought about proffering a sexy invitation, decided if he was interested he would have figured out a way to share the shower with her. "Thanks."

He opened the door a sliver. Laid something on the counter. She peeked around the cloth shower curtain at the pile of clothes he'd placed there. "What's that?"

"A dress Mrs. Adams thinks will fit you, and some girl stuff she'd just picked up for her daughter. She says the dress is her daughter's, and should be a close fit. If you hurry and send her your clothes, she'll wash them for you. For us," he amended. "She seemed concerned that we'd been walking and didn't have what she called the basics of life."

He was thinking of basics and she was thinking about his body. "Thank you, Dante."

"No problem. Mrs. Adams is really nice. She sent us a tray of salad and cold chicken. You hungry?"

For him, yes. "I could stand to eat." She shut off the water, got out, toweled off. Glancing over the clothes, she wasn't crazy about the idea of a dress, but she held it up to her. Actually, the dress wasn't bad. It was a soft cotton with short sleeves, not stylish, but a cute turquoise blue. Comfy for traveling. Wouldn't look entirely horrible with the moccasins Dante had bought her. "Mrs. Adams's daughter must be young?"

"About your age," Dante said cheerfully. "Mrs. Adams said that if you ever decide to kick me to the curb, I'm to come back and let her introduce me to her daughter, Suz. Apparently, Suz is a helluva cook."

"That's just nice," Ana muttered, slipping on the dress. She rinsed out her under things and laid them out to dry. "I'm taking a shower thinking about you, you ape, and you're out trolling for girls."

"Did you say something, cupcake?" he asked through the door.

"No, stud muffin," she replied, ever so sweetly.

He cracked open the door, looked in at her with a big grin. "I thought I heard you say something about a stud muffin. I think that's girl talk for hot, sexy guy, and the only one of those around is me."

"Really." She had no idea how to puncture his oversized ego. "Zip me, please?"

"Glad to help." He reached to zip the dress, came to a complete halt.

"Something wrong?" she asked, her voice concerned and innocent—but since her panties were drying on the counter and the zipper just crested the top of her bare fanny, she had a pretty good idea what had him stuck.

"Uh…no. Nothing at all."

She watched him surreptitiously in the bathroom mirror. He swallowed, then suddenly reached out, zipped her up fast. Jumped out of the bathroom as though he was attached to a rocket. Clapped his Stetson on his head.

"You ready to eat?" Dante asked.

"Sure am," she said cheerily, knowing he'd have to try to eat dinner with her wearing nothing under a soft, pretty dress. She smiled, and he looked cornered, and Ana almost took pity on him.

But, no. If he wanted to play reluctant prince, she could play unattainable princess. Naked-under-this-blue-dress princess. She walked past him, enjoyed his hangdog face of absolute suffering. "Are you all right, Dante?"

"I'm fine. Thanks. At least I think so."

He looked stricken. Cast a fast glance over her body, tried to act as if he wasn't thinking about what he'd just seen. Ana held her breath, enjoying ruffling that famous Callahan ego just a bit.

Maybe tonight this cowboy would overcome his resistance and fall into her arms.

Chapter Four

Ana was going to kill him. Plain and simple, and hardly lifting a finger to do it, Ana St. John was going to give Dante cardiac arrest at the ripe old age of nearly twenty-eight.

Either she was deliberately trying to seduce him, or he just couldn't think about anything but sex around her. Yet it wasn't *just* sex, though he wished it was. He was crazy about this woman, had been for months.

She talked about wanting his child, but he knew she just had baby overload. Ana had spent too much time around Sloan and Kendall's adorable twins, and naturally—quite naturally, in his opinion—she had decided that a baby was what she wanted, too. A child of her own.

The thing was, she'd settled on him—and granted, he was stocked full of testosterone-charged, baby-making potential—but he really wasn't in a position to simply scatter his seed to the wind and then have his little baby mama disappear.

No. He needed some commitment, a relationship, yes, a marriage, before any of his swimmers could be set free to do their wondrous thing. Yet he was not a marrying man…at least, he'd never thought much about it. Hadn't thought about it at all. Ever. Dante sat in the back of Ash's truck, and Ana sat up front, chatting away with his sister, who'd come to their rescue after he'd finally surrendered and realized he had to call for backup.

He'd had no other option, though he believed it would be safer for his family if he and Ana stayed undercover for a while longer. But he could not spend a night in a bed with Ana and not fall into hot, sweet temptation. He was only so much man where she was concerned, and he had to draw a line between him and her that he wouldn't cross.

"Don't you think, Dante?"

His sister's voice jerked him from studying the slope of Ana's shoulder as she sat in the passenger seat, blissfully unaware of his heated admiration of her. Ashlyn's gaze settled on his in the rearview mirror, and he was pretty certain his sister was laughing at him.

"Think what?" he demanded a bit crossly.

"Think that this is all related. Those troublemakers that grabbed you guys are the same ones who did this before. It has to be linked."

He nodded. "Stands to reason."

"Then we go find your uncle Wolf and tell him that enough is enough," Ana said. "No doubt Dante will enjoy beating him to a pulp."

"Uh—" Dante blinked, considered how macho he needed to appear. "We actually don't believe in beating our uncle to a pulp. Well, actually, we might, but Running Bear says no."

"Oh. So you're using your wits instead of weapons. I admire that." Ana turned around to look at him, and he felt himself appreciating for the thousandth time her sexy green eyes. Kind of an emerald tone, a bright forest green overlaid with honey, and he—

"Dante," Ashlyn said, interrupting his heated thoughts, and Ana turned back around. "When's the last time you heard from Tighe?"

"I don't know." He didn't figure he'd thought much about his twin since he'd been in Ana's radius. "We're not joined at the hip."

"That's news to me," Ash said.

"Old news," Dante said. "Tighe's like a cat. He'll come home when he's ready."

"But it's not like him not to check in," Ashlyn pressed, and Dante finally caught his sister's underlying message.

"You think something's happened to him?"

"We don't know what to think. Tighe can be hardheaded, and with you not traveling with him to be the communicator—"

He scowled at his sister's reflection. "Tighe has a mouth that works perfectly fine. I wasn't always the communicator."

"Yes, you were," Ashlyn insisted. "It was always you who kept in touch with the family. We always called Tighe The Silent One. In fact, Galen calls him Silent-but-deadly, and he swears it's because of his work in the military, but it's still rude and I let him know it."

Dante could hear Ana giggling in the front seat. "So was I Not-silent-and-not-deadly?"

"We just called you Oprah," Ash said cheerfully. "We could always count on you to have something to talk about."

Well, wasn't it just nice for his sister to air all his dirty laundry in front of the woman he was dying to impress? The woman who now knew that not only was he not a fighter, a tough guy, but he was considered a hen by his family? "Thanks, I think," he said, and Ana and Ash dissolved in giggles.

He wondered if Ana would rescind her offer to have his child now that his sister had so nicely illustrated the family's views of him. Jace had certainly thrown himself at the nanny bodyguards, but they'd seemed to treat him as everybody's favorite beta-male brother, fun and nonthreatening. "Yes, I'm going to share my new recipe for blackberry pie and drop-stitch knitting tips I got from Mrs. Adams with Aunt Fiona as soon as I get home."

"Oh, don't get your feelings hurt, brother. We love you, you know," Ash said.

"I'm fine. I really got a recipe from Mrs. Adams, and she shared some knitting tips." He smiled, not caring if he did sound too sweet to be a retired SEAL.

Ana turned to look at him. "Her blackberry pie was excellent."

He nodded. "It sure was."

"How did you get clothes for me, and a great recipe and knitting tips out of her?" Ana asked, and he shrugged.

"Dante's a chatterer," Ash chimed in. "He can talk the ears off a rabbit."

"I told you," he said, ignoring his sister. "She liked me. I think she really wants me to come back and check out her daughter."

The smile slipped off Ana's face. "I thought you were just bragging."

"No." He shook his head. "She's a really nice lady, too. I like older ladies. She reminded me of Aunt Fiona.

You can learn a lot from sitting around listening to folks who have more than six decades on them."

"You certainly seemed to learn a lot about her daughter," Ana said.

"Not too much. She's twenty-seven, can cook like a dream, has a goddess body, and Mrs. Adams swears she's not exaggerating, and won a pageant of some kind. I can't remember which one," he said, thinking hard. Pageants weren't something he'd had a whole lot of familiarity with. Ash wasn't the type who'd ever enter a pageant. She probably wouldn't score very well—too ornery.

"Mrs. Adams was fishing for you to ask out her daughter while you were with me?" Ana demanded.

He shrugged. "I told her you were my sister."

Ashlyn laughed out loud.

Ana frowned. "I thought she said that you were to come back and meet her daughter if I ever kicked you to the curb."

"She didn't really say that. I was just trying to get your goat."

"You're getting my goat now," Ana said, and he could hear Ashlyn snickering.

There. That was better. The spotlight was off him. He liked it better when his little doll was worried about him going off with a pageant winner with a mother who made melt-in-your-mouth blackberry pie. "It probably is time to hunt up Uncle Wolf and explain to him that we don't want to hear a peep out of him over the holidays," he told Ashlyn. "Or we'll bury him in a canyon with only a cactus to mark the spot."

"I thought you were a pacifist," Ana said, and Ashlyn shook her head.

"Be careful, Ana," Ashlyn told her, "my brother is a spirit that moves on emotion."

"That's right," Dante said. "How far are we from Hell's Colony, Ash?"

"About thirty minutes. Why?"

"Because we're being followed. Don't turn around. Don't speed up."

"How do you know?" Ana asked.

"I can see the truck we were tossed in. Look in your side mirror, Ana."

"He's right, isn't he?" Ashlyn said. "He's always right. It's like he has a freaky sixth and seventh sense combined."

"He is right," Ana confirmed. "I hadn't noticed." She sounded depressed about her lax bodyguard skills.

"What's the plan, brother?" Ash asked.

"You're going to bypass the road to Hell's Colony. We'll head toward Rancho Diablo instead. How much gas do we have?"

"Half a tank."

"Should be good enough to get us to the border." He reached up to rub Ana's shoulders. "Didn't I say I'd take care of you?"

"Yes," Ana said, "but I should have seen it first."

He grinned. "You girls were too busy chatting to be looking out for such things as rogues and rascals."

"Here it comes," Ash said, "the crowing of the man who wants applause."

Dante leaned back, completely satisfied that he was the hero once again, and not the hen. Well, sometimes the hen, but mostly the hero. "They're following us," he said, "because I left them a note with Mrs. Adams. I had a feeling they'd show up there."

"What are you talking about?" Ana demanded, turning to stare at him, outrage lighting up those fascinating peepers he loved to admire. "Why would you do that?"

"I like to keep my enemy close," Dante said. "Makes every day a bit more exciting."

Ana looked at Ash. "Has he always been insane?"

"Yes," Ash said, "certifiably. I did try to warn you. Now my brother Jace is more of a Steady-Eddy. If that appeals to you."

He grinned at Ana. "In the grand scheme of things, you'd probably prefer excitement to predictable, beautiful."

Ana looked so annoyed he couldn't help laughing. He was so tempted to lean up and give her a hot kiss right on those heart-shaped lips, but the window shattered behind his head, and Dante yelled, "Down!"

"I don't need this much excitement," Ana said from the floorboard, checking the firearm Ash shoved at her from the glove box.

Dante slapped a clip into the gun he grabbed. "I read that women get pregnant more easily when they've been under stress."

"Who told that lie?" Ash demanded, jacking the truck up to about eighty miles an hour. "And who's getting pregnant?"

"No one," Ana said. "I had a momentary lapse in judgment." She glared at Dante before she fired a shot out the back window. A tire blew on the truck, and it veered off the road. A few bullets sprayed after them, but they were too far away for anything to hit.

"Nice," Dante said. "I like a woman who can shoot straight."

Ana looked at him, locked the gun and stored it away again. "Well, I prefer a man who isn't crazy."

"Ah, an impasse," Ashlyn said. "I'm so glad love hasn't come my way yet."

"No, you're not," Dante said, and Ana said, "Who said anything about love?"

He grinned at her. "You know you want me. And I want you. We don't have to bring up love just yet."

"It won't matter." Ana turned back around. "You're free to stay in the wild."

She was miffed. He smiled. That was all right. She'd only stay miffed until he kissed her, and then his little baby-seeking darling would be only too happy to let him charm his way into her bed.

Guaranteed.

DANTE WAS CRAZY. Ashlyn had tried to warn her in the beginning, but blinded by—well, lust didn't sound quite appropriate but definitely desire—what a sexy devil he was, and her hope to have a baby, she'd ignored his sister's warnings.

Now that she'd learned just how wild 'n' woolly Dante was, she realized the error of her ways. Such genes could only lead to her having a wild child of her own, and nothing good could come of that.

She went to the kitchen at Rancho Diablo and found Fiona frowning at a cookbook. Fiona looked up with a smile when she saw Ana.

"Just the person I wanted to see," Fiona said pleasantly, snapping the cookbook closed. "And right in time to give me a break from trying to raise a Yorkshire pudding."

"Raise a Yorkshire pudding?" Ana glanced over the assembled pots and pans Fiona had scattered around her kitchen. "I don't know what that is."

"I'm determined to have Yorkshire pudding for

Thanksgiving. A roast with carrots and potatoes on the side, and an onion," Fiona said, hustling her up the stairs. "But it takes the right touch to raise a pudding properly, and my concentration is shot these days. This will help." She smiled as Ana followed her to a closet in the attic. The attic was a huge room, more of a well-loved storage area and extra living space if needed. There were shelves on practically every wall. Plump cushions sat on window seats. "Now," Fiona said, sitting down, "what's this I hear about you setting your cap for my nephew?"

Fiona tapped a velvet-cushioned seat and Ana reluctantly joined her. "I set my cap, but now it's unset. So there's nothing to worry about."

"Oh, now." Fiona gave her a knowing smile. "A girl doesn't unset her cap that quickly. Does she?"

"She does if the man in question is too much of a—"

Fiona smiled. "Gentleman?"

How could she tell this kindly soul that her nephew was a devil with an incurable wild streak? "I was thinking perhaps of a different word."

"I know." Fiona nodded. "A sweetheart. You feel like you're taking advantage of him." She patted her hand. "Dante is such a good boy. He'd make a fine husband, Ana. Don't feel bad about setting the female trap to catch him. Men really love to be caught, even though they claim they don't."

"Oh, dear." Ana hardly knew what to say. How to explain that since she'd been back to Rancho Diablo—they'd arrived late last night, and Dante had told his brothers of their highway adventure with no great sense of shame for luring their kidnappers right back to them, a story his brothers had enjoyed with great back-thumping and cocky admiration—she realized she'd made a mistake? "Here's the thing, Fiona. Dante's just not my type."

"Not your type?" Fiona looked stunned. "But River says he's been your type for over a year!"

Ana felt a little blush warm her face for the fib. She wasn't about to say that had been all sexual attraction. "Two days in a truck with him changed my mind."

Fiona sniffed. "Ana, don't be scared of how much you care for my nephew. I know you're trying to protect yourself, but he really does have a heart of gold."

And the soul of a wild man. "I'm not looking for a husband. I just wanted a child of my own."

Silence stretched between them for a second. "Dante will never settle for less than marriage, I feel certain, if a child is involved."

"That's completely understandable." Secretly, she wouldn't mind a wedding ring from that hunk. Yet with his reputation for staying wild and free, she wasn't allotting any dreams for marriage.

"So, it's not that my boy is too much of a rascal for you, it's that you're too gidgety for him. That's a first, I must say." Fiona rose, paced around the attic for a moment, then stopped and peered at Ana. "You don't seem like a gidget to me."

"I don't know what a gidget is," Ana said.

"A flighty girl. One who blows around at every wind." Fiona sighed. "There's only one way to know if Dante's the man of your heart or not."

"He's not," Ana assured her. "I mean, I'm not the right woman for him."

"Pooh. You'd hate to throw away your soul mate just because you've got cold feet." She smiled, her face gentle yet determined. "Now let's just pop you into this dress and see what happens." She opened a massive door, in which hung all kinds of plastic-wrapped clothes, and pulled out a white wedding gown.

Ana had heard all about the magic wedding dress. There was no way on the planet she was putting that thing on. She didn't believe in charms or superstitions, but Callahan legend was thick around this place. "I better not, Fiona. I'm not looking for a husband."

"Nonsense! Every woman wants a husband." Fiona looked as if Ana had sprouted an extra head. "And especially a handsome devil like my nephew."

"I don't think—" Ana began, as Fiona dragged the gown from its sparkling wrapping. "I mean—"

"Now, then," Fiona said, hanging the dress in front of a cheval mirror. "You go right ahead. Take your time." She smiled. "I'm going to get back to my Yorkshire pudding."

"But what am I supposed to do?" Ana was a bit cowed by the gown. No way was she putting it on— what if it *was* magic? What if she saw herself in it and decided she wanted to become a bride? Get married?

No. It was all about the baby. When a woman only had one ovary, she didn't have the luxury of wasting her chances on marriage first, then wishing for a pregnancy. "I don't think I—"

"That's just the thing," Fiona said. "You won't have to think. Once you put it on, you'll know for certain."

"Know what for certain?"

"Who your dream man is." Fiona smiled at her, a benign and yet somehow cagey fairy godmother with a lacy lure. "Wouldn't that be lovely?"

"I suppose—"

"You wouldn't risk throwing Dante back into the dating pool if he was your prince. Of course, you'll be terribly disappointed if he isn't your prince, I know,"

Fiona said, her tone sympathetic and sorrowful for Ana's pain in that circumstance, "but at least you'd know, right?"

Ana glanced at the gown, worried. It was a beautiful thing, and the Callahan brides she'd seen wear it had been stunning. Of course it was all Fiona's storytelling, there was no such thing as magic. Just Fiona trying to up her matchmaking score by one more victim.

"In the Irish we say, *an t-adh leat*. Good luck, dear. And don't forget the reason the gown is magic—you will see the face of the man you love, the prince who's the true destiny of your heart. Or at least that's what the Callahan girls have all said, each and every one."

Humming, Fiona went down the stairs. Ana closed her eyes for a moment, debating. It was so silly. The game was to get her in the gown—and probably any wedding dress would do—so she'd start frothing at the mouth to rush to the altar. "I won't fall for it. I can put that on and feel nothing. It's just yards and yards of beautiful white lace and whatever else wedding gown dreams are spun from. No different from a bedsheet or…or a tablecloth. Just white fabric."

She'd been in love with Dante for a long time, though she barely admitted it to herself. She was just careful, that was all, and a careful woman made certain that she chose the right man to father her child.

She could afford no mistakes. Natural caution was what made her an excellent bodyguard. There was still time to back away from the situation if Dante wasn't the man who could make her dreams come true. "In love" wasn't final, it wasn't endless—not yet, not while she could still hold back from falling all the way.

Yet there was a bigger worry, one she wasn't sure she wanted to know the answer to: if Fiona was right—

the story was crazy but Fiona was known to be un-cannily right on many matters—what if the man who appeared to her wasn't Dante?

Maybe it was better not to know if Dante wasn't her dream man.

It would be awful to be in love with a man who wasn't Mr. Right. On the other hand, did she want to know Dante was the man meant to make a magical future with her? Shouldn't that be the surprise that came on secret dreams to both of them?

It almost felt like Dante was defenseless in the face of her participation in Fiona's scheme.

"Pooh," she murmured, "I doubt I see any man at all. Fiona's got more stories than a fortune-teller at the state fair."

Soft, tinkling music reached her ears. She glanced around, wondering if Fiona was piping music up to her to set the mood. "Fiona, I'm not buying your fairy godmother shtick."

The music was pretty, so lilting and spellbinding that Ana finally smiled. Okay, so perhaps Fiona was using all her props to close the deal. It would be fun to try the gown on and throw cold water on the whole tale of magic nonsense.

Fascinated in spite of herself, Ana touched the wed-ding dress, her heart suddenly beating very fast. Shim-mying out of her jeans and top, she stepped into the infamous magic wedding dress that had led so many Callahan brides to their fairy-tale endings.

Closing her eyes so she wouldn't see the dress until it was on her body, Ana slid the whisper-soft, made-from-angels'-wings dress up to her shoulders, feeling for the zipper of the low-waisted back to draw it up, and breathed in a sigh of excited anticipation before opening her eyes.

Chapter Five

The magic wedding dress was cherry-red.

Hot, fiery red.

Ana gasped, staring at herself in the mirror. The gown was fabulous, magical in every sense of the word. But it had turned redder than fire, stunning and alluring, a princess gown of temptation and sin. It was gorgeous in shades of flaming colors that enveloped her and caught the light from the lamps and overhead chandelier.

Every inch of her screamed unadulterated heat.

It was the most beautiful dress she'd ever seen. Fairy-tale to the max—but not bridal in the least. Not unless you were planning on marrying the devil himself.

Speaking of the devil, Ana glanced wildly around, looking for hers. But Dante was nowhere to be seen.

She was alone in the attic. Fiona was wrong. Ana hadn't seen a vision of the man who was meant for her.

She was doomed to be alone. That had to be what this vision was telling her! In spite of the fact that she didn't believe in magic—had only been humoring Fiona, and perhaps her own wistful dreams—the dress had changed itself to a Valentine-ball-fabulous creation of sexy siren seduction—yet there was no dream man to go with it.

Ana looked down, fascinated and horrified by the twinkles and stardust that seemed to burst from every seam of the full skirt.

Dante was not the man of her destiny.

Worse, if the magic wedding dress was right, it looked as if she could be cast as the Code-Red Vampire Bride of Rancho Diablo for next year's Halloween.

She tugged the gown off as fast as she could, replaced it on its hanger, put on her clothes and escaped from Fiona's attic of mumbo jumbo, her heart breaking painfully at her first experience with magic.

"WHOA, WHAT WAS THAT?" Dante peered out the kitchen window, surprised to see Ana hurrying across the yard past the corral, clearly heading back to her house. No doubt it was time for her to be on duty, taking over from River.

"What is what?" Fiona came to stand beside him. "Huh. That's…Ana. Running, and maybe crying."

"I know. The question was rhetorical. What I meant was, why's she running like she's seen a ghost?"

"Uh—"

Dante turned to look at his aunt. She stared up at him, her gaze too innocent even for his delicate aunt. "What did you do, Aunt Fiona?"

"Nothing. I've been in here baking a cinnamon cake, as you full well know."

She returned to gazing out the window, searching the landscape with a bit more interest. An uncomfortable feeling grew inside him at his aunt's worried countenance.

"Should I check on her? Make sure everything's all right?"

"I wouldn't," Fiona said, not looking at him. "You know how women are."

"Sometimes I do, sometimes I don't," he said, considering her, knowing full well she was up to something, yet not certain how to pry it out of her. Fiona was good at concealing things when she wanted to, which was quite often.

"You'll learn in due time, I'm certain," Fiona said, retreating from the window and returning to her baking. But he knew his aunt, and she didn't normally wear a face full of worry. She must know more than she was telling.

He sat down at the counter, reached for a piece of the newly baked cinnamon cake. She popped his hand lightly with a spatula. "You don't have time to snack," Fiona said.

"What better use is there for time than eating your cake?"

She refused to smile. "I don't know. Go find a cow to brand."

"You're going to have to tell me, you know. I can see that something's on your mind. Can't keep these things in." He reached for the cake again, and this time his aunt didn't apply the spatula to him.

"You can't possibly understand," she said, sinking onto the bar stool next to him. "That gown has been part of my family for years. It's never backfired. The magic has always been as strong as that of the Diablo mustangs."

He frowned. "I thought that was Sabrina's dress. That she got it from some Romanian ancestor."

Fiona shrugged. "Romanian, Irish, it's just magic,

isn't it? Does it really matter? It's magic as long as it works." She glanced at the window and let out a deep sigh. "Ten brides and the magic was still alive and well. Something's gone terribly wrong. When the magic goes away, well, it's very, very troubling."

"How do you know any magic has gone away?"

"Because I've never had a female try on the magic wedding dress and run off in tears." Fiona's face was completely woebegone.

Thunderstruck, he glanced toward the window again, almost as if he might see Ana again. There was nothing outside the window but the lengthening fingers of November twilight. "What do you mean, try on the gown? Are you saying you had Ana put on the magic wedding dress?"

His aunt nodded, grabbed a tissue to wipe at her eyes.

"Why?" he demanded. "What made you do that?"

"I don't know," Fiona said. "I was trying to help!"

He didn't like it. Why would Ana be running like something terrible had happened, unless something terrible *had* indeed happened? He was an ex-SEAL; operators didn't run. Ana was a bodyguard. He'd never seen her run unless she was playing tag with the children. Mostly, he'd seen her hold and cuddle Sloan and Kendall's babies Isaiah and Carlos, her hands gentle, her demeanor soothing and loving.

"I'm going to go check on her." He got up, but Fiona put a hand on his arm, stopping him.

"Give it a chance to wear off, nephew."

"What to wear off?" He felt certain he needed to get to Ana immediately, before she completely wrote him off. The way she'd been hauling ass, he wouldn't be surprised if she escaped from Rancho Diablo—and him—*tonight*.

"Magic is very powerful," Fiona began, "and if she had a bad experience—"

"How can that happen? Ten brides put that white thing on and glowed like they were made of diamonds. What makes the dress turn on someone?" He felt a terrible sense of destruction yawing over his heart suddenly, as though the fragile relationship he'd had with Ana might have been dealt a blow from which it might not recover.

"Well, more brides than ten," Fiona said, gulping at some tea. "That gown has been in my family for centuries. It's magic, you see, and magic is timeless—"

"Enough," Dante interrupted. "Get on with what happens when the dress of dreams turns into the rag of doom. I swear, if it's hurt her, I will rip it to shreds and use it for horse wrappings. I'll use it to—"

"Shh!" Fiona looked mortified. "Don't say such things aloud!"

"Why? Can it hear me?" he said it to be sarcastic, but the moment the words left his mouth he wished he'd whispered them.

"Not necessarily *hear* you, but it knows when it's not… I mean, magic has to be believed in, you know, it can't be cheapened with doubt!" Her agitation grew, but so did Dante's. Ana might have just slipped from his grasp—no woman retreated like that unless she wanted to be far, far away from a man—and he didn't care if she wore a potato sack, he just wanted her.

"Whatever," Dante said. "Tell me how to fix it, or I'm going to go kick its man-catching ass, and then take a pair of scissors to it. Right before I toss it into a good hot Christmas-season bonfire!" he yelled at the ceiling where even a dead body in the attic would hear him.

At that, his redoubtable, amazingly stiff-resolved aunt fainted dead away.

"You big lug," Ashlyn whispered to Dante, staring at Fiona as she lay in the bed.

She'd helped Dante get their aunt upstairs to her bedroom, where Burke now fluttered helplessly at his wife's side, muttering, "No worries at all, she'll be fine, she's a stout lass," and not making Dante feel any better at all.

"You can't curse the magic wedding dress," Ash said. "Don't you know better? You don't curse *any* magic. It's seriously bad stuff."

She gave him a frown meant to punctuate her stern words, and it did puncture, practically deflating him. "Wake up, Auntie," he whispered. "I didn't mean to cuss out your—"

"Don't you dare say her illusion of chicanery," Ash said. "I can hear you thinking it, brother. You are disrespecting the very core of Fiona's belief system. What next? You'll stand out in the canyons and shake your fist at the Diablos? Why are we here if we don't believe in the family lore?"

"I don't know anymore." He sank back against the wooden chair he'd appropriated.

"That's because you have no belief." Ash patted Fiona's hand. "You probably lost it in Afghanistan."

"No," Dante said slowly. "I really don't think I ever believed in anything but myself and my family."

Ash's eyes went round. "Don't let Running Bear hear you say that."

He sighed. "Tighe believes in magic. And spirits and

her most glorious. Men remembered skin and darling breasts and heart-shaped derrieres. But Dante would bet if you asked a man what the dress his bride had been wearing looked like five days after she'd worn it, there wasn't one on earth who could tell you half a detail about it except that it might have been white. Maybe.

But that same man would be able to go on for a year yakking about how great it had been to kiss every inch of his bride's—

The gown shimmered at him, waking him from his sudden burst of imaginings of Ana's bare softness. Miles and miles of satiny skin and shy curves—

He shook his head. Glanced at the thing again, wondering if it was taunting him with frosty white luminosity, daring him to touch it. "I have to put you back in your bag," he told it. "You've caused quite enough trouble for one day. And I have to say, why you had to pick on my lady, I really don't know. Were ten Callahan brides your limit? Did you run out of magic?"

The gown was hardly a fitting foe, troublesome rag that it was. And it really didn't deserve his animosity, even if it had made Ana cry. Sighing, he reached for the hanger.

To his astonishment, the gown filtered away, disappearing into the thin Rancho Diablo air that existed, indeed lived for, mysticism and tales of legend. He waited, astonished, his blood pounding.

Chapter Six

He was in all kinds of trouble.

Dante replaced the hanger and tried to assess what he was doing in his doughty aunt's attic with a disappearing dress. "If you could reappear, you'd make my life a lot easier," he said out loud, mainly to calm his racing heart.

Nothing.

He sank into a window seat and pondered what to do next. SEALs assessed, they didn't panic. He had an upset lady on his hands, who had tangled with the supposed magical purveyor of happy wedding dreams. Obviously that scenario hadn't gone well, not to mention that her sweet attempt at seducing him had ended with them both trussed in the back of a pickup, and that had hardly been the stuff of a woman's fantasies. He had a gown that had hit the road—or air—and that wasn't going to go well when he had to go downstairs and put in the report to Fiona. "Nuts. I'm beginning to get cranky," he muttered, stating the obvious to himself, which didn't help much.

Apparently, the lesson was that everything was out of control at the moment, no different from when he'd been on top of Firefreak, hanging on for dear life and preservation of limb. He'd survive this, as he'd survived more dire circumstances in his life. But things had gotten sticky. Dante got up, grabbed the plastic cover that was supposed to protect the magic wedding gown, zipped the bag up and shoved it back into the closet. The bag hung limply, devoid of its charmed contents. Shaking his head, he turned off the lights and went downstairs to check on his aunt.

She sat in bed, surrounded by adoring family. Her silver-white hair was pulled back in an elegant coil, and she wore a gray lace dressing gown that made her look like a queen holding court, though that court was just his brothers—the family jesters—and his capable sister.

"Here's my able-bodied nephew," Fiona said. "Did you take care of it, Dante? I know you did, I don't even have to ask. You've never messed up a mission." She smiled, trusting him.

Was it worth upsetting her? The regal aunt still looked so pale. Maybe it was best to wait until she was stronger to mention that her treasured mystical apparel had shazamed. On the other hand, perhaps he'd better just suck it up and confess that there was a great chance he'd offended the gown with his cursing, and it had hustled back to magic land. Fiona looked at him expectantly, confident that her nephew would have taken care of the matter as a Callahan did, with efficiency and thoroughness. Ash blinked at him, wondering at his hesitation. Jace frowned, Galen raised his brows, and Tighe— "Hey, twin. When did you get here?" Dante demanded, shocked to see his brother.

"About five minutes ago, and clearly not a moment too soon." He glared at Dante. "I let you go off on your own, and apparently you've lost your mind."

"Probably." He thought about the gown and shook his head. "I've got it together more than I look like I do."

Tighe didn't look convinced. "I stopped by to see River. Apparently, Ana packed up, gave notice and headed out."

"What?" All his confidence slid away. Dante stared around at the pitying expressions of his family, painfully aware that they thought he was the equivalent of the classroom dolt. "She can't be gone! She would never leave those little boys, she loves them…" He let his voice trail off as the faces staring at him became even more sorrowful. "Where did she go?"

"We don't know," Fiona said.

Ash came to tuck her head onto his shoulder, and though her silent support was bracing, it was horrible that everyone felt so sorry for him. *I'm gone for her, I knew I was crazy about Ana, and everybody else did, too, except Ana.*

Maybe that was for the best.

"Well, I guess Ana did what she had to." He thought his tone sounded quite practical. "Women. Who can predict what they'll do?"

That remark didn't draw him anything but puzzled stares. Dante decided to head off with the shreds of his dignity hanging in tatters but at least still partly available to him. "Glad you're feeling better, Aunt Fiona. I'm sorry for the trouble I caused." He kissed her cheek.

She grabbed his hand. "You did make sure the gown was tucked away carefully?"

He couldn't lie. He just couldn't. Never had, didn't plan to start now. "Aunt Fiona, the dress disappeared."

"Disappeared?" She looked at him, her lower lip

trembling slightly. "What do you mean? Did Ana borrow it?"

"I don't think so." He patted Fiona's hand. "It just simply filtered away."

She blinked. "Oh, *disappeared,* disappeared. I see."

She didn't see, and he didn't, either. His aunt probably thought he'd exacted his revenge on the evanescent cloth, as he'd threatened. Gowns just didn't vanish into the ozone, nothing did, not really, and so, he'd gone from hero to heel in a fraction of a second.

Fiona released his hand and leaned back against the snow-white pillows again. She looked somehow more fragile than she had just thirty seconds before. He glanced around at his family, who didn't hide their disappointed expressions.

There was only so much a man could take.

"I'm going out for a while," Dante said, departing to the relative safety of anywhere but Rancho Diablo.

THE OBVIOUS THING to do was to go talk to River. Ana's friend and colleague would know more than anybody about what had upset Ana enough to make her leave her precocious, adorable charges. Dante decided he had nothing to lose by stopping in to see if he could dislodge any information from the woman who had given his twin little to no encouragement.

Tighe was in the same boat he was—a sinking boat—though his brother didn't seem to know it yet.

He knocked on the door. River opened it with Sloan and Kendall's two toddlers hanging on to her, precious with their wide eyes and wondering expressions.

"Hi, Dante," River said. "Your twin just came by. Busy day at the ranch, huh?"

"I guess." He waited until she waved him inside. "I heard Ana might have gone out for a bit."

She knelt on the floor to stack blocks with the kids. "It's true. We have a sub coming in a couple of hours."

"A substitute bodyguard?"

"Absolutely. Sloan would never allow Kendall and the kids to stay here unless they were completely covered, especially not after what happened in Hell's Colony with the sniper getting hit and all. And of course you and Ana getting dragged off."

His many transgressions were stacking up on him. "I guess I'm not exactly dream-date material."

She smiled. "Probably not."

There was little he could do about that. Rancho Diablo was a hot location; it was impossible to predict from where the next attack could come.

"If it makes you feel any better," River said, "Ana did say that the night she spent with you was amazing."

Amazing, hell. They hadn't made love, hadn't kissed. She'd know amazing when he finally got her in his arms. He shoved his hat back on his head. "Do you know why Ana left?"

"There's only so much I feel I can tell."

She'd actually said more than he'd expected her to. "I understand. Thank you." He'd been left with the consolation prize that the woman he had a major thing for at least thought he had potential.

Although not enough to not give him up.

"This might sound strange, but did Ana tell you if she'd tried on Fiona's magic wedding dress?" What woman ran from a dress? Weren't ladies generally more inclined to knock down everyone in their path to get the perfect gown on their body and a man to the altar?

River looked confused. "She didn't mention it. Isn't that dress a Diablo fairy tale?"

It was impossible that River didn't know of the Callahan family legend. Dante studied her, wondering if she was stringing him along, but then his cute nephews toddled over and struggled to get in his lap, and he grinned. "Got new trucks, guys?"

He admired their new toys and they stared up at him with big navy Callahan eyes. "I have a funny feeling Ana's going to miss you terribly, gentlemen."

"That's exactly what she said when she left," River said. "In fact, they're a big reason Ana realized she couldn't stay here any longer."

He glanced up at River, intrigued by the information she was divulging. "What do you mean?"

River went into the kitchen and began making little plates of snacks for the boys. "Ana said she'd gotten too attached. What started out as a simple bodyguard position turned into a lot more."

Dante kissed his diminutive nephews on their heads. Ana had been with them about a year, since before Sloan had married Kendall. Too headstrong to be sent off away from her husband forever, Kendall had returned with her own security detail, Ana and River, who pretended to be nannies but were actually in charge of protecting the twins. The lines had been blurred a long time ago as Ana and River really enjoyed being with the children and part of the Callahan family. They took their job very seriously. Dante was completely comfortable with Ana and River overseeing the safety of his nephews. "I can understand how Ana could fall for these little guys. They'd steal anybody's hearts."

"Yeah." River looked away for a moment. "Occupational hazard. Ana's totally professional, though. She wouldn't have left only because she cared too much about the boys. She left," River said, hesitating, "because she'd begun to want a child of her own. Very much."

Dante blinked. Felt a little ball of excitement lodge inside him. Heck, if she really wanted a child that badly, he'd be more than happy to give her one. The thought was so strong as it came to him that he tensed, worried for a moment that he'd spoken his thought out loud. It had been so real. Of course he'd love to have a child with her. "Sounds pretty normal to me. Doesn't it to you?" If he hung around these little guys most of the time, he'd want a child, too.

He *did* want a child.

Dante swallowed hard. That was a new thought. He noted River hadn't answered his rhetorical question, but he sped on, his curiosity prodding him. "So, nothing happened that involved an enchanted dress?"

River shook her head. "Not that she mentioned. She was upset when she came home, but she's been planning to give her notice ever since you two got back from…you know."

"She's been planning to leave since the Halloween thing?" That was two weeks ago. Dante's heart clenched up, tightening his chest.

River nodded. "Ana took it very personally that she hadn't been able to stop the kidnapping. She felt like she hadn't checked your room out thoroughly enough. And felt guilty that it could have been these little boys who got taken instead of the two of you. Carelessness isn't good in our line of work." River's expression was so sad that Dante felt for her, and for Ana, too.

"It wasn't her fault. It was an ambush." It had been

his focus that was entirely distracted by the lady who'd shockingly appeared in his bed.

"It's the job of a bodyguard to secure a location." River shrugged. "Ana felt she'd gotten too close to her job."

"You mean she thought she'd gotten too close to me."

"And the boys." River set the snacks on the coffee table and reached out to smooth a hand over each small head. "Between wanting a child so badly, and letting an attacker get past her, it was time for her to move to another position. She gave notice as soon as you two returned from your unplanned trip."

His brain felt Firefreaked. Ana wanted a child, she thought she was at fault because a kidnapper had gotten inside his room, she and the magic wedding gown had clearly not taken to each other—

"Ana doesn't think she can have a child," River said. "There's a possibility she can't, anyway."

Dante braced himself. "Anything you can share?"

"I probably shouldn't, but maybe you should know. She had what was diagnosed as endometriosis in her early twenties. The doctors thought they could solve the problem since it appeared to be confined to one ovary. She's very worried about her chances to have a child with only one ovary. The doctor didn't seem all that optimistic."

He rose. "Thanks for telling me." It didn't really faze him. He'd never had a problem hitting targets. "Any idea where she went?"

"Home."

Dante kissed each of his nephews goodbye, giving them each a last, fond hug. "Where's home?"

"South Dakota."

Great. "Don't tell me. She didn't hail from a hot spot of commerce and nightlife."

She laughed. "I'm afraid it's a bit more remote than that. Ever heard of Buffalo Gap?"

"Nope." Didn't matter.

He could find it.

Tighe walked in without knocking, and the boys ambled over to his brother with surprisingly steady steps. Then one sat down on his diaper hard, and Tighe scooped up his brother, knowing that would set the one on his bottom to scrambling to his feet in order to be held, as well.

"Don't make them competitive, Tighe," Dante said.

"Competition makes the world go round. We cut our teeth on it." He laughed when his tiny nephew gained his feet and grabbed him up in his other arm. "You boys like me better than Uncle Dante, don't you?"

Dante noticed River's face had taken on a becoming pinkness as she watched Tighe strut his father potential stuff. Disgusting. "Haven't had a chance to ask you what got you off the circuit, bro."

Tighe glanced at River. "Heard you'd gotten yourself into a small scrape. Figured you needed me. Robin can't operate without Batman, you know. I'm Batman, obviously." He grinned at River with his natural swagger and ease of braggadocio.

Dante snorted. "Thanks for the vote of confidence." There was another reason—or other reasons—his brother had returned, but clearly those were a topic for a more private audience.

"You weren't there for our aunt's announcement. I told her I'd swing by and let you know what's on her mind. Just so you know, she's not too happy you did something with her wedding dress." Tighe looked at him with utter sorrow. "Really, man, it's beneath you. If you're afraid to get married, just say so and don't hide the aunt's lucky charm."

Dante shook his head. "Can you give her announcement to me in shorthand instead of the long, windy version?"

Tighe grinned, sent a wink River's way. Dante thought his twin was laying it on just a touch thick, but who was he to quibble? At least Tighe seemed to have a captive audience, while Dante's audience—Ana—had flown the proverbial coop. "Sure thing. Now that you're playing dirty pool with the fated frock, Aunt Fiona decided she'd go ahead and let you know that unless the gown is returned by Christmas, she's pulling the plug on your portion of the ranch raffle."

"I didn't do anything to the stupid dress."

River drifted out of the room with the boys and Tighe watched her go with obvious reluctance. "I do believe I'm making headway, bro."

"Whatever you have to tell yourself." Dante sighed. "Focus. You're wearing me out with minutiae. I prefer my action to be all of a piece, not death by paper cuts."

Tighe went to the fridge and selected a beer for himself. "Then she got to rambling. Said she and Burke had planned to buy that ranch north of here, and that Chief Running Bear had been on board with the plan of enlarging the Rancho Diablo footprint. But she's had second thoughts. Says we're probably stretched too thin, and that everything needs to calm down for a while before she considers taking on more ranch land."

Dante's gaze widened. "Fiona made this decision just because her dress disappeared?"

"It might have been the last straw. She says too many things are going awry, that the hands aren't steady on the plow anymore. I think she means us. Mainly, she's madder than a wet hen at you."

"I figured." Dante sank onto the sofa arm, pondering his brother's news. "Oh, well, live by the sword, die by the sword."

"Exactly."

"Personally, that suits me fine." He didn't like the whole marriage-for-acreage scenario, but he would have loved getting the ranch. He'd hoped it would be him who would win the raffle, simply because he'd long dreamed of a place to call his own. He hadn't really envisioned a family with him there, though. Frowning, Dante realized he'd secretly hoped Ana would want to live with him, here in the circle of the Callahan closeness.

Yet she'd gone back to South Dakota without even a blink. "If our aunt ends the ranch raffle, Sloan and Falcon are in a bit of an awkward place. They got married."

Tighe smiled. "They're getting a consolation prize."

"What is it?"

"Big chunks of Dark Diablo, in Tempest, New Mexico. I've only been out there a couple of times, but it's a jewel."

Dante nodded. "I know. It's beautiful."

"Jonas Callahan was generous about the parcels he offered them. Frankly, I wish I'd gotten to the altar in time for that sweet deal."

"I never had plans to get to any altar until I met Ana. Now the thought doesn't totally horrify me."

"Won't matter if you love the idea like a puppy loves a bone, bro. Fiona says you're not getting one grain of dirt from this ranch until you bring her dress back. Further, she's not sanctifying any marriage or children or anything. You know, Aunt Fiona sounded serious, and I've never heard her speak of marrying us off in anything but glowing terms. Now everybody's mad at you. Including me, I guess. Really puts a crimp in my bachelor status not to have a shot at the ranch. I was planning on using that bait to my advantage. However, I am a bit more competitive than you are, as we know."

Dante didn't wholly care that he wouldn't get any land. He was extremely bothered that his adorable aunt was upset with him. "I didn't do anything with her dress, Tighe, I give you my oath on that. The silly thing just went…poof."

Tighe snapped his fingers. "Just like that. Right after Ana tried it on, and you were supposed to put it away." His brother winked. "Now, listen, bro, we all know you're a little skittish when it comes to spending more than one night with a beautiful lady, repeats have never been your thing and certainly romance isn't your—"

"Tighe," Dante said, interrupting with purpose, "I would never sabotage Fiona, or Ana, or anybody. I don't believe in magic. At least I didn't." He shook his head, still shocked by what had happened to him in the attic. "I just can't imagine what Ana saw to make her run like that."

"You didn't say anything about a running bride." Tighe looked at him expectantly.

"First of all," Dante said as patiently as he could, because clearly his brother had taken one too many rings to the bell when he'd been on the circuit, "there was no running bride."

"You said yourself that Ana tried on the dress, and then she ran away. That makes her a bride on the run, if you ask me."

"No," Dante said, even more patiently, "I never

asked Ana to marry me. I don't know why she was trying on Fiona's fabled gown."

"Fiona said that Ana had asked about the dress. Said she had heard all the Callahan brides had worn it." Tighe smiled as if his brother were the slow one. "That means Ana must have believed on some level that somebody might eventually proffer her a proposal. And everybody knows that Callahans need brides in order to get the new ranch. Or at least we did, until Fiona changed her mind 'cause you made her mad. Upset her something fierce. Never saw her that upset, Dante, truly. That gown is part and parcel of our aunt. You better return it on the double, is my advice, and I hope you'll take it." Tighe looked at him with a rather pitying, disgusted expression, having decided that his brother lacked honesty and core principles to steal a woman's dress and do something heinous to it. "Anyway, the point is, Ana doesn't know you don't need a bride anymore. I bet she'd come back if she did know."

Dante blinked at his twin's circular thinking. Compared it to the mental notes River had given him. "Are you saying that in your august opinion, Ana left because she didn't want to marry me?"

"My guess is she thought about it, briefly toyed with the idea, as women do from time to time. But then she put on the gown and just couldn't envision herself taking the walk of happy endings with you waiting at the altar for her. Maybe she saw you as more of a gargoyle than a prince."

"Okay. That's all I can take today. I'm off." Dante headed to the door.

"I'd go with you, keep you company, help you hold your head up. I know how tough it is to take a smack down from a woman you're hot for." Tighe nodded as if he knew the secrets to the universe. "I know you came home for her, man. I wish like hell it had worked out for you."

Dante left, not sure what had just happened to him. He was in the doghouse with everyone. His brother's boneheaded pity was just about the final ounce of humiliation he could swallow.

It was time to hit the hay and plot his next logical course of action. Until Tighe had started yapping he'd been certain his next stop was South Dakota. River had him convinced all Ana needed was sweet words of reassurance.

But then Tighe had sowed seeds of doubt Dante was sure he'd be wise to consider, if not heed. What woman wanted a man to follow her, track her down, try to sway her—when the last thing she wanted was to ever see him again?

He needed his bed in the worst way, and about ten hours of uninterrupted sleep. Maybe his subconscious would reward him in the night with the answer, because he sure as hell was out of any.

The bunkhouse was dark. The dark sky was lit by a huge hanging moon of brilliant white, a winter moon rising, to his mind. Perfectly serene and silent in a wide sky of black nothingness, which was just about how his brain felt right now.

He pushed open the front door. A lamp was burning in the kitchen, so he detoured that way and grabbed a glass of water, gulping it down. Briefly, he considered the medicine cabinet his brothers tossed various tonics and crapola into on occasion. Grabbed a couple Advil and washed them down with a slug of whiskey, telling himself one or the other medicinal approaches would surely work on the pounding headache he'd developed.

What had happened to that cursed dress, anyway? He was still a bit freaked out over that. And Ana? Had she run from him? Could he be as much of a sad sack as Tighe, imagining something that wasn't there at all?

He considered taking the whiskey to his room, to give the Advil a chaser until it worked. Picked it up, set it back down, shrugged. All he needed was sleep.

He opened his bedroom door and saw Ana sound asleep on top of the denim coverlet. Her blond hair fell over her shoulders, her black sweater clung to darling breasts, her hips in dark jeans half-turned toward the ceiling.

The headache and sleepiness disappeared just as the wedding gown had. He looked at the gift in his bed and felt as awake as the morning sun.

Sleep was overrated. Way overrated.

He had much better things to do.

Chapter Seven

This time he wasn't going to mess up. And he sure wasn't going to let the moment slip away again. He crossed to the bed. "Ana."

She opened her eyes. "Hi."

"You all right?"

She smiled. "Yes. And no."

God, she was beautiful. He was indeed as lost as Tighe. Could he hang himself out on the ledge again without giving her a chance to get there with him? No. "Heard you were heading back to South Dakota."

"Sure thought about it." She watched him, her eyes luminous and soft in the lamp's gentle light. "Hope you don't mind I came here instead."

He swept a golden strand away from her face. The feeling hadn't changed for him. He still felt like an angel had dropped right into his bed, on loan from heaven. He was pretty certain that he could marry this woman, if he was the marrying kind, and fifty years from now he'd still feel like heaven had gifted him with something amazing and extraordinary.

He sank onto the bed. "So now what? You got a flight out in the morning?"

She shook her head. "I wanted to talk to you first."

"About?"

"I wanted you to know some things."

She was in the mood to talk. This was good. At least he thought it was. It would be much more to his liking if she was in the mood to try seducing him again, because he sure would let her. Right? He wasn't that big a dummy to let her slip through his hands twice. "I'm listening."

"Okay. Dante—"

He waited, letting her take her time.

"I've kind of had a little thing for you for a while." She watched to see how that registered with him.

"A little thing?" He'd been hoping for a big thing. He sure had a big thing for her.

"I feel like if we'd met in another time—"

This wasn't good. This was the kill-you-with-kindness goodbye. He'd heard about these, and they were killers on the man, who was supposed to be left with his ego intact but instead ended up with his heart shattered.

He wasn't going there. Ana opened her mouth, and Dante didn't let her get one more word out. He kissed that goodbye right off her lips, and then he proceeded to show her just how he felt about her, inch by glorious inch.

ANA AWAKENED IN THE NIGHT, realizing Dante was wound around her. She smiled—for a moment. It was amazing being with Dante, just as she'd known it would be.

"Hey," Dante said to her, nuzzling her neck, "why are you awake?"

"I need to go," Ana said, curling into his arms.

"I thought we discussed that." He kissed down her neck, settling in the curve of her throat.

"Did we?" It was hard to think with Dante kissing her. Wild, sensual emotions swept her, making her wish for things that couldn't be.

"Mmm. I made love to you, and you liked it."

"I did." She kissed him back, falling a little further in love with him.

"And so you decided that taking off for parts unknown was not in your best interest. You realized there were things around here you'd miss too much to leave." He moved over her, and Ana's breath caught.

"There are things I like," Ana said, and Dante said, "I'm going to give you something else to consider before you make your final decision about leaving," and then he was making love to her, and Ana let herself get lost in the moment.

"HERE'S THE DEAL," DANTE said as dawn broke over the New Mexico skies. "You stay here at Rancho Diablo. I'll do my best every day to convince you that I'm the man for you." He kissed her hand, raising it to his lips, working his angle. Surely Ana knew that they belonged together. Whatever had spooked her could easily be solved.

She leaned up to kiss him goodbye, then reached for the bag she'd neatly packed. "I have to go, Dante."

More convincing was needed. "I know in my heart you want to stay. I can feel it every time I touch you, lady. You like me."

He pulled her to him. She smiled and stepped away, shaking her head. Dante didn't allow himself to consider defeat—he knew Ana was crazy about him. No woman made love to a man the way Ana did with him and honestly believed she wasn't in love.

No. Not just in love. She was crazy for him, just as much as he was for her.

It was the baby thing bugging her, he knew it had to be. Trouble was, a guy just couldn't come right out and say, "Hey, I heard you have one ovary and are worried you can't have children, but I can fix that for you if you give me a shot." No, a man had to be more suave than that. He was suave.

At least he thought he was. "Marry me."

He surprised both of them by saying it. But he felt great the moment he said it. Ana's eyes widened, and he thought *bingo, that was the right thing to say.*

But then she shook her head, sending his world into dust. "I can't, Dante. You don't understand. I— It wouldn't work. We're not right for each other."

"You're exactly right for me." He wasn't going to let her go until he'd told her how he felt about her. Then if she still said no—well, he wasn't going to think about it. Better to imagine a *yes* coming from those sweet lips.

"Dante, it's hard to explain. I don't think—"

If she was going to be like this, he'd just play along with it. So he pulled her outside and helped her into his truck.

"What are we doing?" Ana asked.

"Taking a drive. I'll drive, you talk. Things come to me when I drive. I'm determined to help you see that you don't want to leave me in the pond, gorgeous."

"I'm not leaving you, Dante. I'm taking myself away from the pond."

"Every woman fishes for a man. At least that's what I heard. And I'm pretty sure I've got bait you like."

She didn't reply, but that was all right. He drove to the end of the canyons, parked the truck. A wide panorama of beautiful, undulating gorges and walls carved by time lay before them. "Come on."

She got out of the truck. "Where are we going?"

"To the most romantic spot on earth. At least I think this is romantic." He supposed maybe not everyone thought the canyons were as beautiful as he did. But he really loved it here, more than any place he'd ever been. "I'm going to try to change your mind. Be lightly warned."

She didn't protest when he took her hand. "Here's the deal, gorgeous. I know something's bugging you. Why don't you tell ol' Dante? I'm known as a problem solver."

She let him pull her against his chest, and he ran a comforting hand down her back.

"You can't solve any of this."

"Consider me your knight in shining armor." He kissed her, lingering against her lips. "And this knight really wants you to be his lady."

"Dante," Ana said, "you're not the man for me."

He looked at her. "You can't say that after last night. I'm pretty sure I know the sound and feel of a happy woman."

"I know beyond a shadow of a doubt that you're not the man for me."

This sounded off. There was a hidden message he couldn't decipher. He took her over to a canyon ledge that jutted slightly out over the gorge and tugged her down next to him. "This is beautiful," Ana said, staring at the amazing, mysterious landscape.

"It is."

Why did the canyons sing to his soul? There was something lonely and yet alive, too, about them. He always felt most alive here. "Much better than South Dakota, I'm sure."

She laughed. "You don't know that. I love my little town."

"I can live in South Dakota, if you're not keen on being here," he said, struck by the sudden thought that maybe he was in the wrong place. Heck, he was a traveling man—he could go where she wanted to.

"Dante," Ana said slowly, "I tried on the magic wedding dress that your aunt Fiona—"

"I knew it!" Dante turned to stare at her. "You were crying when you left the house the other day! Because you'd tried on that thing!"

"I wasn't crying exactly—"

"I know, I know, bodyguards don't cry. Okay, so you had sun in your eye. What happened up in that attic? Because when I went up there, everything looked just fine to me." At least for a couple of minutes, anyway. But he wasn't about to share that. "So you actually put the dress on?"

She nodded, and his face split into a grin. "You like me, Ana St. John, you're crazy about me, and you want me like chocolate cake. You wouldn't have been trying out the fit of the magic wedding dress if you weren't thinking about me."

Ana looked away. "It's not very gentlemanly for a man to crow about a woman's feelings."

"Oh, I'm crowing, all right. I'm going to crow louder." He pulled her into his lap, kissing her until she was breathless. "You're just dragging this out. I am your knight in shining armor, and I think you know it."

She moved back out of his lap. "Actually, you're not, Dante. I didn't see you when I put the gown on."

"Of course you didn't, doll. I didn't go up there

until you'd left." He saw no problem with that whatsoever. "But if I'd known you wanted me around, I'd sure have been there." He frowned, struck by a thought. "I thought it was bad luck for a man to see a woman in a wedding gown. There's some superstition about that. I think it's like a black cat crossing your path. You don't want to see a woman in a wedding dress, at least if you're a die-hard bachelor. I believe that if you see a bride, you might end up with one." He considered the notion. "Of course, I'm okay with that. I don't believe much in magic and superstition, and elves and gnomes and fairies and things."

She shook her head at him. "You don't understand. I didn't see you."

Oh. She was trying to tell him this was about her and not him. He supposed he was a bit of an attention hog; he'd been trying to figure out the wedding gown thing from the guy's perspective. "Like I said, I wasn't there. But if you want to put it on again, like, next Saturday, I'll be there with my best jeans and dress jacket on." He was pretty hopeful he could convince her. She belonged to him, and vice versa, he just had to close the deal. Wipe away whatever cute little female worries and oogie-boogies were bugging her. It was the man's role, and he was good at that. "So, Saturday? We can send the jet for your family. I heard my cousin Rafe just updated his aircraft."

This was easier than he'd thought it was going to be. If all she was worked up about was the gown, they could fix that. He'd thought it was the baby-making problem—and if that had been her issue, he'd been prepared to do a little bargaining.

She put her palms on either side of his face and stared into his eyes. "Dante, the legend of the magic wedding dress is that a woman is supposed to see the man of her dreams, the only man for her, when she puts it on."

He took her hands in his, kissed them, thinking madly. Okay, now he had a problem because he hadn't heard that angle. "That's just some of Fiona's mumbo jumbo." But he wasn't certain. The damn dress had disappeared from his hands. He couldn't dismiss that. "I wouldn't worry your pretty head about that if I was you."

She gave him a look of disgust. "I'm not worrying my pretty head, thank you. You're doing all the worrying. What I'm telling you is that you are not my prince."

"Huh. I swear I never thought a woman would ever say that to me." He didn't like it, either. "And to think I thought you were holding back for a baby."

She blinked. "A baby?"

"Yeah. I thought you wanted a child and wasn't sure I was up to the task." But he felt icy fingers of fear jab at him. If Ana hadn't seen him—and though he wasn't one to go in for nonsense, Fiona's nonsense sometimes had kick—maybe he couldn't give her a child.

And that was what she wanted more than anything.

"I do want a child."

"Very normal for a woman your age and in your circumstances."

"Which are?"

"You know." He waved a dismissive hand, wanting to get back to the problem at hand. This subject was leading them down the wrong path. "Hanging out with the Callahans is enough to drive any woman to want a child. The place is just chock-full of hormones. And you're closer to thirty than twenty. Even I've started dreaming of a baby bootie Christmas, and trust me, I never wanted a kid before."

"It's not about my age, thank you."

The ire in her voice bypassed him as a horrible thought arose in his mind. He sat up straight. "Hey, you didn't see another man, did you?"

"I—"

He looked at her intently, his heart jumping around. "Did you?"

"Well," Ana said slowly, not meeting his gaze, "yes, I did, as a matter of fact."

HE HAD TO LET ANA GO, in the end. There was nothing else to do. She hadn't seen him when she'd tried on the dress—stupid rag, he should have burned it or made a quilt out of it, and if it ever returned, he was going to make that garment regret its fairy-tale shenanigans.

He hadn't had the heart—or the guts—to tell Ana that the story was even worse—that when he'd actually been in the same room with the thing, it had disappeared.

Left him holding the plastic bag it belonged in, actually.

He hadn't dared to confess that he and the gown had bad karma. Matters were certainly dicier than he'd expected. So he took her to the airport and said goodbye, his heart tearing into a thousand shreds.

He might have tried to overrule the idea of a wedding dress governed by magical intentions, except it was gone. So he clearly had to let the woman of his dreams go.

But it just felt wrong. In his heart, he knew Ana and he were magical together. Wasn't that all that mattered?

Maybe not in the mystical world that was Rancho Diablo. But he'd never in his wildest imaginings thought that a woman would leave him because of a spellbound gown.

He went home to face his aunt, who no doubt remained upset that he was responsible for the destruction of her treasured heirloom. He was out of the ranch raffle—no chance for that now. But that wasn't what he'd change in a heartbeat, if he could.

He'd change magic into marriage.

Chapter Eight

When Dante returned, Chief Running Bear sat in the kitchen snacking, and no doubt plotting, with Fiona. "Hello, grandfather," Dante said. "Haven't seen you in a long time."

Lately the chief showed up more often than the once-a-year at Christmas his Callahan cousins claimed was his pattern before. Maybe it was because there was more family here for Running Bear to juggle. If there was anything his grandfather and aunt lived for, it was steering the family ship.

The chief nodded. "We have much to discuss."

"What's on your mind?" Dante sat on a bar stool next to his grandfather and gratefully accepted the hot coffee and thick chocolate chip cookies Fiona slid his way. "Thank you, Aunt Fiona."

"You're in the doghouse with me, nephew," she said, sailing off out the door.

"Whew." Dante drank the coffee, shook his head. "That is one unhappy aunt."

Running Bear sipped his tea and said, "You cursed the magic."

"I—" Yes, he had. He'd sat in this very kitchen and

hollered unkind words up the stairs. "Look, I've never been a big believer in tchotchkes and thingamabobs."

His grandfather nodded. "I know."

"And I really don't believe that the dress disappeared. It had to have been an optical illusion." His resolved stiffened. "Fiona has a lot of tricks in her very deep bag."

Running Bear shook his head. "Do not doubt the unseen."

"Yeah, well." What could a man do? He had faith—he did, otherwise he wouldn't have survived the dry, endless days of war he'd experienced. "Dresses just don't disappear. But I'm sorry Aunt Fiona is upset."

"What about your woman?"

Dante sighed, didn't try to pretend he didn't know what his uncle was talking about. "Ana left. Said I wasn't the right man for her."

"She had a vision."

"I don't really—" Dante nodded. "Okay, she did have something like that. At least she said she did. Whatever happened, it really spooked her." He remembered her running past the window. He'd known she was crying. "I don't believe in visions and spectral heebie-jeebies. But I do know that Ana's vision was real to her."

"Yes. You weren't in it. She had an empty vision."

"Not for lack of trying on my part."

"Do you know what happened?"

Dante shook his head. "She said she hadn't seen me. She said she saw another dude, but I'm not sure if she was just trying to throw me off. If there really were some other man, I think I would have…"

"Would have what?"

He'd started to say, *I would have lost my mind,* but

he was made of sterner stuff than to lose his cerebral advantage over a rival. "Well, I would have told her man that I wasn't giving her up."

"Yet you weren't in her vision."

"Yeah." Dante studied his coffee. Then the picture went crystal clear. "Oh, hell! You're trying to tell me that she didn't see me because she didn't want to! She doesn't believe that I'm her heart's desire, or her perfect prince, or whatever!" He looked at his uncle triumphantly. "Because she doesn't believe it in her *heart*." He leaned toward his uncle, his voice conspiratorial. "Have the Callahan brides figured out the trick?"

"Trick?" Running Bear looked at him with puzzlement in his dark eyes.

"Yeah. The Callahan brides see the man of their dreams because they *want* to." This was so simple! Fiona had cooked up the perfect autosuggestive story to set the Callahan ladies' hearts to fluttering with imaginary conjurings of what they wanted. "So all I have to do is convince her, and then Ana will try the dress on again, and she'll see me." He felt very good about figuring this all out except for one tiny, terrible detail. "But the dress is gone. Didn't even leave behind an enchanted thread I could—hell, I don't know—whisper pleas and prayers over."

"More like you should whisper something else," Running Bear said, standing.

Dante raised a brow. "Such as?"

His grandfather shrugged, grabbed a cookie for the road. "You're not suggesting I apologize to a dress, are you? Because that's really… I mean, that's further out on a limb than my imagination can take me." He was so confused he didn't know what to think.

"We shall see many things in the future here," his

grandfather said. "Saying goodbye is easy. Maybe other words are more difficult."

He left, closing the kitchen door behind him. Dante got up to follow, opening the door just in time to feel a whoosh of air as a dark black shadow raced past him, galloping toward the canyons and disappearing into the night.

His grandfather had been riding a black Diablo mustang.

Which was crazy, because spirit horses were just… spirits. And yet, spirits were the heartbeat of Rancho Diablo. Why had he said he didn't believe in mystical things? He was surrounded by them.

Because he'd lost that faith when he'd been fighting, and was no longer that innocent youth who'd gone off to war.

And yet he knew better, in spite of himself.

His grandfather had tried to hand him the key to the puzzle. Somehow, the lock was just out of Dante's reach.

"I CAN'T FALL FOR DANTE," Ana told her mother, Lynn, as she helped clean the small store her parents owned in Buffalo Gap. "Not more than I already have, anyway. I promised myself I would never get married. At least not until I was a bit older. I like my career, and I don't want that to change. Truthfully, I never wanted to have to tell a man I had a female issue that might affect our marriage." She hadn't wanted to be defective—as a bodyguard, strength was her calling card. She thought about all of this for a minute while sweeping the dust from the floor into a dustpan. "Dante is the kind of man women dream of. Dark and handsome and strong. Intelligent. Courteous."

Lynn smiled. "You're in love."

"I am. I just don't want to be."

"So you're here until you get over it." Lynn moved some pies and cakes onto the counter, placing them under glass covers. "You can stay as long as you want. I can use the help." She looked up with a smile. "You've been here three weeks. I'm glad you finally want to talk about it. I was beginning to worry."

Ana was so glad to be home. Of course it was the Christmas season now at Rancho Diablo. Fiona would be deep into the festivities, stringing her lights, baking up a storm. The ranch took on a glow of romantic beauty that was all its own. "I do miss the ranch, and the Callahans," Ana said wistfully, thinking about the little twins she'd been trusted to protect. "Those are the most adorable little boys. I guess they'll really be walking a lot now."

Lynn smiled. "Your father needs help putting up the wreaths. Make sure he gets the ribbons straight, will you?"

"I will," Ana said, but then she knew it was time to finish telling her mother the truth. "Mom, I'm expecting."

Lynn hugged her. "I know, honey."

Tears popped into Ana's eyes. "How did you know?"

"Well, the lack of appetite was either love or morning sickness or both. The ginger ale you've been drinking signaled that I was going to be a grandmother. Your father and I have been about to burst waiting for you to tell us."

"I don't know what to do, Mom. I'm so happy. Shocked, but happy. I really believed I would have much more of a problem getting pregnant."

"Well, sweetie, when one doesn't use protection—"

"Oh, we did. Trust me, Dante is a man who leaves nothing to chance. Although I didn't tell him I couldn't have a baby." Ana enjoyed her mother stroking her hair for another moment, and then stepped away. "I always felt so guilty that I was an only child and I might not be able to give you grandchildren."

Lynn smiled. "I know. I figured it would happen when the time was right. And it appears that the time is right, now."

Maybe it was. She didn't know. "I don't know how I'm going to tell Dante that the condoms were defective."

"From what you tell me, he seems like a pretty confident man. Something tells me he may not be all that shocked, and will even love bragging about it." She put a hand over her heart. "You need to tell your father. It's been driving him mad, not being able to say anything. We didn't want to ask too many questions." Lynn's eyes twinkled. "But here's a little secret that may interest you. Your father bought a new pony. He's in the corral, waiting to be named by the new bundle of joy."

Ana couldn't help smiling. "I love you, Mom. And Dad."

"We love you, too. No matter what you decide, we support you."

Ana went to help her father and give him the good news. As she passed the window, she glanced outside, spying a tall, muscular cowboy on the street. Her heart jumped, and she looked closer, but of course it wasn't Dante.

She was surprised how fervently she'd wished that her Callahan cowboy had come to get her.

"IT WAS A LARK, REALLY," Fiona said. "I didn't mean to cause trouble by having Ana try on the wedding dress! I was attempting to be helpful." She sat next to Chief Running Bear on the hood of the military jeep she used often on the ranch. They perused the canyons, companionable from knowing each other so long. "I felt certain she'd see Dante and realize that he was the man for her!"

"Get another."

Fiona gasped. "Another magic wedding gown? Where would I get one of those? They don't exactly grow on cacti!"

He shrugged. "It's the legend the brides loved. That's the magic they believed."

Fiona blinked. "Are you saying I should buy just any old wedding dress, and tell the Callahan brides it's magic?"

"Is there another way?"

"Yes," Fiona said, "my mischievous nephew can tell me where he hid it. He's not getting one single acre of that ranch land until he does!"

"We didn't purchase the twenty thousand acres," Running Bear reminded her. "You might recall the farmer decided not to sell. To us."

"The boys and Ash don't know that," Fiona muttered. "I have no problem spinning that web as long as I can. And that farmer may decide to sell eventually."

"My son Wolf put too much pressure on the farmer to sell. Wolf wants that land so he can legitimately stay close to Callahan land, wait for the right moment to strike."

Fiona's blood chilled. "It's never going to work. He's never going to find your other two sons and their wives. Jeremiah and Molly and Carlos and Julia are forever safe."

"Wolf has a long memory. He's paid well by the cartel. He is my black sheep, and has no intention of being anything else. He has time to wait for the right moment."

"I'm so sorry," Fiona murmured. "We always hope our kids will grow up and be productive people with character. I wish he'd fall into a hole!"

Running Bear laughed ruefully. "I don't understand his choices. We are like night and day."

They stared off for a while, neither speaking. Fiona worried, more than she wanted to let on. "Some days I wonder if it would be easier if we sold the ranch and started over elsewhere. Colorado, even Montana. Texas."

He patted her hand. "I know, old friend. We must believe. We are on the side of right."

"But maybe right doesn't save us." Fiona felt a heaviness that seemed to suffocate her sometimes. "Although I've always believed that good guys win, sometimes I wonder if we're passing a heckuva legacy to all the little Callahans." She looked at Running Bear. "They don't know Jeremiah and Molly, and Carlos and Julia. Maybe they'll wish they didn't have to always fight so hard to keep the family secrets safe."

Running Bear shook his head. "Callahans are strong. We know what we're fighting for, and we'll teach the little ones. As we did before."

He meant with the six Callahans she'd raised here, for her sister, Molly, and Molly's husband, Jeremiah. Why Wolf wanted to kill his own brother—Jeremiah— so badly was something she'd never understand. How could one turn on his brother and hope to sell him out to the enemy?

It all went back to the days of blackness on the land, when the cartel tried to take over. Jeremiah had fought back, and Molly had believed in that fight. Carlos and Julia had joined in, and now their seven kids were here, fighting for the land. For family, for community. For a way of existence no one else could understand, maybe, unless they'd lived with the same ancestors that had breathed life into them. "Wolf should have known. He was one of us."

"Everyone chooses their path in life. Greed overtook him." Running Bear sounded very sad about this, and Fiona patted his hand, as he'd comforted her. "But no, I never think about giving up. You're tired, old friend. Yet you are strong. Wild tigers couldn't make you give up one inch of this land."

"I know. I'm grumpy today. Things didn't work out between Dante and Ana the way I'd hoped they would. Dante did something to my magic wedding dress, and that's enough to put any woman in a stew. And I feel like something's not right around here." She looked around. "Maybe I'm getting old."

"We have many years behind us," Running Bear agreed, "but you're feeling the changes that are coming."

Fiona perked up. "Changes?"

He nodded. "Wolf intimidated the rancher to the north into not selling to us. So your neighbor Storm Cash has bought that property."

That meant Cash had ranches on two sides of them. "That's better than Wolf buying it."

"I hope so. We will wait and see."

"A long time ago, I did some horse trading with

Storm. He seemed like an honest person. We talked about going into business together on some horse breeding. Never happened, though," Fiona reflected. "We lost touch for a while. Then he bought the land near Rancho Diablo, and I haven't talked to him much."

"We'll watch him closely, now that we have him at our head and side," Running Bear said, and Fiona sighed.

"That sounded ominous."

He looked at the sky. "Storms are coming. We should get back. I don't want your nephews worrying about you. Or Ashlyn yelling at me for keeping you out too long."

Fiona smiled. Her nephews and niece were very protective of her. "I think I'll stir up some trouble. That will shake off my blues."

"Trouble?" They walked toward the jeep.

"Yes. Since Dante isn't solving anything with Ana—he made a rare mess of that—and besides, I'm annoyed with him, so I'll focus on his twin. Tighe is due for a settling. Especially since he thinks he's become big man on the rodeo circuit."

Running Bear laughed. "What will you do to him?"

"Get him married off, of course. He just needs a little prod. And the best prod I know is a woman. The best way to get a woman—River—to set her cap is to dangle him in front of other females. I managed his brothers, Sloan and Falcon, in very deft fashion, if I do say so myself." The memory made her smile, all the more because babies had once again bloomed at Rancho Diablo. "I'll put up a new sign advertising the hottest cowboy in Rancho Diablo for charity." She smiled with satisfaction. "Our charity raffles have been outrageously successful for my beloved Books'n'Bingo Society. With the last raffle, even after we paid off the sign bill, we cleared fifteen grand. Plenty to donate for new paint and toys for the children's wing of the hospital."

"I'll help in any way I can," Running Bear said, his eyes twinkling.

"Good," Fiona said. "Get yourself dressed up for the Christmas party I'm having in the town square. You'll need a costume." She looked at him. "Maybe a pirate?"

He shook his head. But he laughed, and Fiona finally smiled. "You won't know it's me when you see me," he told her. "Get ready, old friend. I can be mysterious."

Fiona sighed with happiness as he drove the jeep toward home. A masquerade Christmas party was just the thing to lift her spirits.

But first, she had to enlist some help. Wrangling nephews was not easy, and backup was essential.

Chapter Nine

"That's an easy one," Mavis Night said. "Kiss a Cowboy for Christmas."

The three ladies sitting around the table in the Books'n'Bingo Society tearoom and bookshop looked at Fiona to gauge her reaction to the idea for a new woman-luring slogan. "Needs more energy, I think."

"More sex appeal," Corinne Abernathy said, and Nadine Waters giggled.

"More sex in general," Nadine countered.

Fiona's three plotting friends studied their notes again.

"Win a Cowboy for Christmas," Corinne said. "That's the point, after all, of our charity raffle."

"No sex, though, and Fiona likes sex," Nadine said, and Fiona knew she was being gently teased.

"Only in its proper place," Fiona said, and her friends gave her mirthful glances. "Sexy sells. What woman doesn't love a rugged man with charm and courage?"

"Ana St. John," Mavis said, making Fiona frown.

"We're not concentrating on Dante's problem right now," she said.

"I don't see why we don't just set the bull's-eye right

on Dante. You said you're annoyed with him, and that he and Ana are splitsville. Serve him right if we set him up to be swarmed by a hive of honeys."

"I did have high hopes that beautiful girl would tame Dante," Fiona said. "I really like Ana. She's a tough, smart lady. Dante needs tough and smart to counter all that testosterone."

They sipped their tea, taking a break to let the wheels turn.

"I say tying him down is your best revenge for his mischief," Nadine said. "Besides, he's such a sweet guy. I've always had a fancy for men with long dark hair and a sexy growl."

"When did he growl at you, Nadine?" Corinne asked, her blue eyes agog behind her polka-dotted glasses.

"Gracious!" Nadine glared at her dear friend. "Dante never growled at me! I was thinking of something else entirely!"

"Really?" Fiona asked curiously. This was a side of her friend she didn't know. "Who growled at you and had long hair—who wasn't in your dreams, of course?"

Nadine leaned close. "Well, if you must know, I ran into John Wayne once, in costume, in a very small town in Texas. He was dressed as a scout, and he was ever so handsome." Her gaze went dreamy. "Of course, that man was my idea of hunky, in costume or out of it, or just in the dark."

They blinked at her, completely astonished.

"And he *growled* at you?" Mavis looked as if she might faint with delight.

The door opened before Nadine could finish her tale. Dante strolled in, his two small nephews in his arms. "Customers for you, ladies," Dante said. "The guys bribed me into a cookie."

Fiona looked at one of her favorite nephews. In spite of her ire, she had quite the tender spot for Dante. "*They* bribed you? Or you used them as an excuse?"

He kissed all the ladies, and the boys squirmed down so they could get hugs. This was a well-established routine, and if Fiona had anything to do about it, every single Callahan born on the ranch would quickly learn that here, kisses and cookies were doled out to sweet great-nieces and great-nephews who paid visits to their aunt's shop.

But this nephew hadn't earned his way out of the doghouse yet. She leveled a sour look at Dante. "No cookies for you, Dante."

"Why? There weren't any left in the kitchen by the time I got in from chores. I think Ashlyn might have sneaked them off to Xav Phillips." He shrugged. "I can't find her anywhere, and that usually means she's in the canyons paying a call on her elusive cowboy."

"Speaking of those wily, elusive cowboy creatures," Fiona said drily, "we are hatching a plan to get your twin hooked. So leave the boys with us and shove off for a bit. We have plans to make."

Dante looked amused. "Does Tighe know you're setting a trap for him?"

"Of course not," Fiona said. "That would give him a chance to avoid the bait."

Dante edged himself into a chair at the table carefully, eyeing the four ladies with some approbation. "Why not Jace?"

"He's not ripe yet," Fiona said. "Too green for the picking."

"What about Galen?"

"He's got a lot on his mind. I don't think he could focus on a woman right now. The trap-ee must be in the proper frame of mind. Receptive, willing and not paying full attention to possible influence."

"Not Ash," Dante murmured. "She's determined to wear down Xav one day."

"Not likely any time soon," Fiona said, "but let us not digress from those who need a kick start."

"We notice you haven't mentioned yourself," Nadine said with a sweet smile, and Dante shook his head.

"No, ma'am. I'm going back to rodeo right after Christmas."

Fiona's jaw dropped. "Why, for heaven's sakes?"

"I should never have come back here." Dante pushed his hat back. "I came home to see if—"

"To see if you could change Ana's mind," Fiona said softly. "Oh, Dante, I am so sorry."

"Nothing to be sorry about." He smiled as his nephews were each given a small sugar cookie, which they held, staring with interest, before slowly putting the cookies in their mouths.

"And you're giving up just like that?" Corinne looked curious and slid him the cookie plate.

"The lady made her choice." Dante took a soft piece of gingerbread, happily munching it as if he had little on his mind but his stomach, Fiona thought with some righteous disgust. They chatted awhile longer, and Dante snagged a few more cookies, then got up and collected his nephews. "Anyway, Aunt Fiona, about your matchmaking."

"Yes?" she asked carefully.

"There's nothing worse than someone who keeps hanging around when the other party has declared themselves unwilling. I hope you won't be upset that I'm returning to the circuit."

"Well, I am surprised," Fiona said, not admitting that she was closer to discouraged.

"It is true," Mavis said, "that when a lady tells a man no, she means it."

Fiona glared at her friend. Mavis was not helping! Who cared if Ana had said no? Was Mavis suggesting that Dante lacked sufficient grit and gristle to wait out the storms of a woman's affections?

But Ana hadn't seemed all that stormy. In fact, she'd been a girl whose feet were always on the ground.

Dante knew that, too.

"Yes, ma'am, I've always believed a woman's words were to be taken at face value." Dante looked around. "Thank you, ladies, for the visit. It's always good to see you."

"Let me get you a roadie box," Fiona said quickly, jumping up to fill a box with assorted cookies for her big, strong nephew. He'd quite melted her heart with his story of unrequited love! Was there anything more heartbreaking than a man who had his heart set on a woman who didn't return that affection? It happened all the time, certainly—but this was her kin. He'd find someone else one day, but she'd really believed Ana was the woman for him.

Yet Ana hadn't seen Dante when she'd tried on the magic wedding gown. "I should have meddled better," Fiona muttered to herself, and took the box to Dante. She leaned up to give him a quick hug. "I think she's crazy not to reel you in, nephew."

"Thanks, Aunt Fiona." He looked a bit embarrassed at her fond words, and Fiona told herself that, luckily for Dante, she held the wand that could shower him with affectionate females who weren't so stupid as to not fall head over heels in love with him.

"I was thinking about swinging by and picking up some hamburgers to grill out tonight for the clan, since you're working so hard here."

"Ohhh," the ladies all said, delighted with his courtesy, and Fiona felt the last vestiges of her anger with her nephew slip away for good.

"I've got some wonderful corn on the cob put by, if you'd like some," Nadine offered. "Wouldn't that go nicely with grilled hamburgers?"

"That's very nice. We'll take it." He grinned at all the ladies, raffish and a rascal to the max. "I'll come by and grab it from you later. Bye, ladies."

The door closed behind him, and every woman sighed.

"That is one long, tall drink of very handsome water," Corinne said.

"I don't know how you grow 'em so big and strong, Fiona, but they always seem to flourish at Rancho Diablo," Mavis agreed.

"Lots of cookies and milk," Fiona said, and then it hit her. "Ladies, we're going to have to go for a twofer."

"Twofer?" Corinne asked.

"We're going to have to raffle both of them," Fiona said. "They've been together all their lives. Tighe and Dante should go down together. I just can't leave my dearest nephew out of the fun. It would be unkind."

Corinne nodded. "We'll do the same barn advertising that we did for Taylor, Falcon's wife, and may I just say that I wasn't convinced we'd ever get those two to jump into the marriage nest?" She looked satisfied at the result. "But we did. And we can help Dante get over Ana."

"Yes. Indeed." Although Fiona wasn't so sure about that. He'd been awfully smitten with the bodyguard. "They do say that time is the great healer."

"They say," Mavis said, "that the way to get over someone is find a new someone."

"Absolutely," Nadine said. "So here's the gambit." She put her hands in the air dramatically, and intoned, *"Want a sexy cowboy for Christmas? Diablo's got the twin hunks of your dreams!"*

"Oh, that's catnip," Corinne said. "We'll be swamped!"

Fiona leaned back in her chair. "It almost seems cruel to do it to him. But I did think Dante seemed a bit sad to be left out, didn't you?"

They all solemnly nodded.

"Tighe and Dante are very competitive," Fiona said, and a smile lit her face. "We'll do it! After all, what's the worst thing that could happen?"

DANTE DEPOSITED HIS nephews with River and went to hunt up his sister. He could safely tell her about the plan Fiona was about to launch on Tighe, and they could have a good laugh about it. There was just about nothing more fun than laughing at his cocky, sweet-talking brother.

River hadn't given Tighe the time of day. Dante had discovered that quite by accident. All this bragging Tighe had been doing about him romancing River had been quite the fable. But then Dante had discovered that River was dating a guy over in Tempest and considered Tighe as something of a loose canon.

"Smart girl," Dante said, and headed to the canyon

ledge he knew Xav happened to frequent most. Where Xav was, he'd probably find Ashlyn.

Sure enough, there they were, just as he'd expected—both of them tied and blindfolded, bound back-to-back. "Holy crap!" Dante said, quickly untying them. His blood went straight to boil as his realized Ash had a bruise on one cheek. Xav didn't look like he'd been captured easily, either. "Who did this?"

Xav got to his feet and lifted Ash gently to hers. They dusted themselves off, and Ashlyn rubbed her wrists to get the blood flow back. Anger flooded Dante so sharply he couldn't remember the last time he'd ever felt rage so deep and hot.

Afghanistan. Yes, he remembered well.

"We're not sure. They wore dark masks," Ash said.

"Like the Lone Ranger?" Dante asked.

"Pretty much." Xav looked out over the ledge into the canyons. "I heard them say they'd be back. Let's vamoose."

"You two go ahead. I think I'll hang around and chew the fat with them," Dante said. He had nothing else better to do today than raise a little hell.

"No!" Ashlyn stood her ground. "If you're staying, I'm staying."

"Xav, take my sister back to the ranch," Dante said.

Xav nodded. "Come on, Ashlyn."

"I'm not leaving," Ash said stubbornly. "You can't do this without backup. I'm *backup*."

"I may have been used to legal filings as my weapon of choice as the co-owner of Gil Phillips, Inc." Xav smiled at Dante. "But that was my life before I met you Callahans. I'm staying with her. I guess that makes me backup, too."

Dante stared Xav down. "I wouldn't have thought you were the kind of man to endanger a woman."

"I'm not a woman, I'm your sister. Don't be sexist," Ash snapped. "Give me one of those guns you're packing. You can't shoot them all. I want a few."

Maybe this was a bad idea. Perhaps it would be best to tell his sister and Xav that he'd go back to the ranch with them, and then double back later when they weren't watching.

"And don't think you can dump me at home and then sneak back here," Ash said. "I was the one who got tied up, I have something to say to those birdbrains! I'm tired of getting pushed around." ·

Xav looked at Dante. "Maybe this is a foolish thing to do when she's mad. Low risk/reward scenario with your aunt if Ash comes home with a trophy or two."

"You have a point." Aunt Fiona really looked on Ash as a daughter, and one she was determined was destined to be the next sweet, delicate, butter-doesn't-melt-in-her-mouth debutante of Diablo. Right now his sister looked as if she could clear out a large hornets' nest with a glare. "Just for the sake of conversation, how many birdbrains were there?"

"Seven," Ash said. "But that's just fine because you're packing heat with clips. Hand one over."

"Seven?" He frowned. "You two got jumped by seven men?"

"One less and we would've had 'em." Xav pointed at Ashlyn. "Remind me never to tick her off. She's a fighter."

Seven thugs. There'd been only four before: Uncle Wolf, two female fighters and what Dante thought of as a lackey.

There were seven Callahans.

"Seven's my lucky number," Dante murmured. Something important had shifted in Wolf's plans for Rancho Diablo. He needed to get Ash home before Wolf's team reappeared. It had to be Wolf. No one else would be so bold, so tenacious. "Let's head back."

"Why?" Ashlyn demanded. "We can take them, Dante! Let them know that Callahans are nothing to be messed with!"

"Another day, another time." What if Ana had come here with Ashlyn? The two women had been known to do it; Ash was under strict orders from Galen never to go to the canyons alone, so she'd enlisted Ana as backup on occasion. That was something he'd discuss with his sister later. Right now, the fact that Wolf was adding to his force was a sign of gathering dark clouds. Dante needed to make certain he could think past the anger—he had to be calm and cool. Dante jerked his head at Xav. "Let's go."

Xav gathered up his bedroll, canteen and other equipment. Ash watched him in disbelief, then rounded on her brother.

"You sound like Running Bear," Ash complained, following them. "Existential is not attractive on you. I prefer a little more edge and fight in my brothers."

"That's okay, little sister. You've got enough for the whole family tree."

Ash didn't protest again, and they left the ledge and got in his truck. She hopped in the front seat next to him, and Xav got in the back. Dante added Xav to the list of people he wanted to pick a bone with, mainly to find out if the man had any intentions toward his sister—not that Ash would thank him for butting into her business. Scanning the horizon for snipers, and praying his luck would hold until he got his spirited sister back to the ranch, Dante drove away.

It was time he had a chat with the lately elusive Storm Cash.

Chapter Ten

To Dante's shock, Ana was sitting in Fiona's kitchen when he, Ash and Xav returned. He tried to appear cool, collected.

He wasn't. Not by half.

"Howdy," he said to Ana, as if she'd only been gone a day and not weeks. An early Christmas gift for him, hopefully. *Which reminds me, I've got until the fat man in red shows up to find that stupid gown, or I'm permanently out of the ranch raffle with the good aunt.*

No gown, and no girlfriend. Seven new arrivals to make our lives hell, thanks to Wolf.

At least Ana came back.

He felt good about that, until he realized Ana probably either missed her little charges, or had second thoughts about giving up her position as bodyguard. Her return likely had little to do with him, which was not a good thought.

Never one to hold back, Ashlyn threw her arms around Ana, giving her an enthusiastic hug, which Dante longed to do himself.

Xav slid his gaze over to Dante to check his reaction. The man smirked.

That's okay. You're in no better shape, pal. "Beer?"

he asked Xav, determined to act like an arrow hadn't just landed in his heart at the sight of Ana.

Ana turned to Dante. "Hi, Dante."

He nodded, asked politely if she'd had a good trip, then pasted himself into a corner of the kitchen where he could nurse his beer and observe Ana unnoticed. She'd wanted out and she'd left, no matter how much he'd tried to convince her that she wanted to be here with him. Anyway, she hadn't so much as smiled at him, and a man knew that a woman dug him when she smiled as if he was a god everytime she saw him.

He felt pretty mortal at the moment.

Fiona sailed into the kitchen, greeting Ana with enthusiasm. "You made it!"

"You knew Ana was coming?" Dante asked. Seemed like the least his aunt could have done was inform him.

"Of course. I know everything, nephew, you should know that by now," Fiona said. "You look like the trip was easy on you, Ana."

"Thank you, yes, Fiona," Ana said. "And I saw the new billboard outside of town. I'm assuming there's a lot I can do to help with the Christmas ball this weekend."

"Hang on," Dante said. "Are you back for good?"

Ana hesitated. "I'm going to be staying with River."

"Huh." That had been fairly ambiguous. She hadn't said, *I'm taking back my old job.* Or *I missed the little boys and wanted to be in on the nanny act.*

"There is a lot you can do to help me," Fiona said quickly to cover Dante's brusqueness. "We have over one hundred guests attending! It's going to be a blow-out!"

"I'm certain," Ana said. "Twin cowboy hunks should bring in the ladies."

Dante raised his head. He'd been covertly study-ing Ana's ankles and delicate feet in Christmas-red pumps, but a siren went off inside him at the words *twin cowboy hunks*.

"Twins? Who are you sticking in the mousetrap, Aunt Fiona?"

"Mercy, Dante!" Fiona laughed. "No need to be so suspicious! The elementary school needs a new roof, and that's expensive, so I thought the best way to bring in dough—lots of dough—was to offer two of my won-derful nephews as dates," she said with an apologetic glance at Ana. "Of course, when I ordered the billboard and offered twin cowboy hunks, I had no idea you'd be returning, Ana."

Ana's gaze was clear. "I'm not certain what that has to do with me, Fiona. You have a big party every Christmas. And someone is always the prize, either for a mistletoe kiss or a dream date."

Dante had heard enough. "Aunt Fiona, if I'm the twin you're shilling, count me out." Holy smokes, Ana acted as if he didn't care if he went boot-scooting with another woman or not. How was that for a boost to a man's ego?

Stunk on ice, actually.

"Anyway, I can't. I'm going to be gone until Christ-mas," he said suddenly, making up his mind on the spot. "Xav and Ashlyn were tied up in the canyons when I visited them a while ago." Everyone gasped, and Dante was grateful to have his mind on a problem he could solve—like bandits—and not on a problem he couldn't fix, which was Ana.

If she was over him, that was all fine and good, but he wasn't over her in the least. Just seeing her again made his heart beat like a drum in a Christmas parade.

"Are you all right?" Fiona demanded, rushing over to Ash to inspect her. "You're hurt! Why didn't you say something instead of listening to Dante argue with me about him being the charity prize?"

"Wait," Dante said, "I'm no charity prize. I'm a grand prize."

"Really?" Fiona's face glowed with delight. "I'm so glad to hear it! I'll have that painted on the billboard immediately! The gal who does the billboards for us can be up there in a jif to write Grand Prize on it! Thank you for your generous contribution, nephew!"

"Anything to one-up Tighe," Ashlyn said, and Fiona said, "Come over here and let me put ice on that. Are you hurt, Xav? What happened?"

"I'm fine," Xav said. "I should have been paying better attention. I take full responsibility."

Dante could practically see Fiona's antennae quivering, which was great, because it took her laser-focus off of him, and he could get back to sneaking glances at Ana.

"Oh?" Fiona said. "Did something interesting have your attention, Xav?"

Dante leaned back against the counter, enjoying Xav's pained expression. "Yes, Xav, what had obscured your attention?"

"I don't exactly recall," Xav said, "but I won't let my guard down again. I promise you that. No one will get past me. Consider me the fire wall."

"I'm going out for a while," Dante said, and everyone turned to look at him.

"Why?" Fiona said. "You never 'go out' at this time of the evening. You hang around the house bugging me and eating me out of house and home."

"Change of routine tonight." He tipped his hat to

the gathering at large, tried not to glance at Ana one last time as he walked out. He'd just be satisfying his eyeballs.

"I'll walk out with you," Ana said, stunning him as she hopped off the chair.

"Sure. Fine." He waited while she grabbed her coat, and after saying goodbye, they walked out. "It's going to snow tonight."

"So I heard. I came back just in time."

He assumed she was planning to head over to see River and the boys, so he stayed glued to the spot, waited to see what was on her mind.

"Dante," she said, "I hope it won't be awkward that I'm here."

"Not at all." It would be, but he planned to man up. Clearly the lady hadn't been all that enthralled with his lovemaking—which was strange because he'd rather thought she was. He'd certainly been completely wowed with making love to her, but there was no telling with women. If he were a fish, he was pretty much on the hook, waiting for her to reel the line in. If she wasn't, well, he was still hooked.

He'd survive, and try not to do much dangling on the hook, generating schmuck points from his brothers and sister.

"I'm glad," Ana said. "I'm staying through the holidays. River wants to go home to see her family, and I told Kendall and Sloan I'd be glad to watch the boys."

"That means you'll go to Fiona's shindig." He shook his head. "Hope you brought your costume. It's a fancy dress masquerade."

"I came prepared."

"I'm just going to toss on a fresh shirt and call myself dressed. It's good to see you, Ana. I'm heading back to rodeo after the holidays myself, but I'm sure our paths will cross." Okay, hopefully that took the awkward out of everything. He nodded and headed off, wishing his heart didn't feel as though it was leaking out of his chest. She was gorgeous, more beautiful than he remembered, damn it, and he was only a guy head over heels.

But there were reasons not to get too sidetracked. Look at that poor sap Xav. Somehow some bad hombres had gotten to him and Ashlyn. Clearly he'd allowed Ashlyn to lose his focus for some reason— although Dante realized his sister could make a saint lose focus.

Anything was better than sitting around knowing that the object of his heart's desire was only a few hundred feet away—and she obviously hadn't come back to Rancho Diablo for *him*. So he was headed toward Storm Cash's house to see what trouble he could stir up.

He couldn't afford to lose focus the way Xav had.

"I HAVE A COSTUME," Ana said, as she and River put the boys down for the night. "I'm going as Mrs. Claus."

"That's funny." River kissed both boys on their heads and backed out of the nursery. "Kendall said you were welcome to stay as long as you like, by the way. For good, if you change your mind. She's expecting the new bodyguard sometime this week, so you can help me show her the ropes."

A stab of pain shot into Ana at the idea of someone else taking over her duties, but there was no reason to feel that way. She likely only had another month until she began to show. Right now what was saving her were the sweaters and jackets she wore in the cold weather. "I'll do whatever I can to help her learn what she needs to know."

River glanced at her as they went out to the den and settled on the sofas. "So I thought maybe you came back for Dante."

Ana shook her head. "I knew when I left that we weren't meant to be together."

"It's true he's not exactly the marrying kind." River sighed. "Those Callahans eat, drink and sleep commitment avoidance."

Ana nodded. And what man wanted to know that his condom had been faulty? After Christmas, before he went back to the circuit, she'd tell him. They'd go their separate ways, and all would be just fine. "I miss the little guys. When you and I took this job, I thought, bodyguarding babies, piece of cake. But it wasn't," she said, "because eventually they grow up, or you have to move on to the next job. And that's really hard on the heart, isn't it?"

River's eyes were soft. "I knew you'd miss them. How do you stay away?"

"Apparently, I don't." She'd come back to tell Dante about the pregnancy but it was almost impossible to imagine actually doing it. She'd have to leave here, leave him, leave the children. Everything would change forever—and she so desperately wanted her own child to grow up here at Rancho Diablo, among these wonderful people. *That's how I know I got way too involved with my job.* "What do you think happened to Xav and Ash?"

"I don't know. Everything's been weird around here. I stay with the kids every single second because I'm so nervous something might happen. How easy would it be to take off with little fellows who can't talk and don't know what's going on?" River shuddered. "Running Bear's been hanging around, muttering about darkness and ill winds. The guys try to act like everything's calm and they've got the whole thing under control, but every few months something like this crops up, and I make sure I'm ready for anything."

Ana shivered. "I always worried about Dante. All the Callahans are brave, but Dante's not afraid of anything, almost dangerously. There's no telling what he'll do if he ever catches who's behind the attacks."

"Believe me, I feel the same way about Tighe. I just keep my focus on these little guys, and try to believe everything will work out one day. It will." She smiled. "Here's some gossip. I floated a little fib that I was dating a guy in Tempest so Tighe wouldn't think I had a thing for him. Which I do, as you know. It really wasn't so much of a fib, because I did have a date, and Galen asked me if I had a guy, and I said *hopefully.* It was an ambiguous question, right? Because I wasn't about to say I hoped that guy would be Tighe." Her face lit up with a smile. "The strange thing is, ever since Tighe's been back, it seems like he's been hanging around a lot, in spite of my supposed boyfriend."

"Really?" Ana's brows rose. "Maybe he's the kind of man who likes a little competition."

"Did you see the advertisement Fiona and her gang of matchmakers put up outside of town?" River rolled her eyes.

"About the charity raffle? Hubba-hubba-hunk?" Ana shrugged, trying to act as if it didn't matter to her that Dante was the supposed Grand Prize. "Those boys are putty in their aunt's hands. Whatever she wants, they gladly do."

"They love her. It's all fine by me," River said, "because I'm going to win the date with Tighe."

"You are?"

"Of course I am. And you should win Dante! Then we could double-date!"

She was past the point of luring her cowboy. She was going to be the mother of Dante's child—somehow it seemed she'd gone past the catch-him-if-you-can phase. "I don't think so."

"But why? He should be very intrigued by a Mrs. Claus costume. Although you do know it's a fancy dress masquerade ball?"

"I didn't know," Ana said. "Now that you mention it, I think Dante did say that, but—" She hadn't been listening because she couldn't hear over the racing of her heart. "I don't have a fancy dress."

"Too bad," River said. "Get one! Tighe and Dante are going to wear their tuxes, and they'll be hot as pistols, I assure you. The ladies will go mad. All those ladies will be so jealous when I walk off with my prize!"

"I'll watch Carlos and Isaiah that night," Ana said. She wasn't about to go buy a gown for one event, especially for an event where the father of her child would be auctioned off to another woman. "I will happily babysit the twins."

"No, you won't," River said, "because Fiona is sending all the children off to Hell's Colony that night. Jonas and Sabrina and all the clan out there have offered to take care of the little guys. Rafe's picking them up in the jet the night before. So you have no excuse not to go!"

Oh, she had an excuse, one that made her smile everytime she thought about it. She loved being pregnant, she couldn't wait to be a mother and hold her own baby.

But that didn't mean she wanted to see Dante walk off with another woman, and think about all that went along with a night with him and an eager female. "Do you think it's best to give a man news he's not really expecting before or after big events in his life?"

River coughed on her tea and set her glass down on the table with a whoop. "You're pregnant!" She practically leaped over the coffee table and landed on Ana, hugging her with ecstatic giggles.

The door opened and Tighe walked in, grinning at their celebration. "Can I play, too?"

"No, you can't," River said. "Go away."

"I always wondered what girls did when they were alone together. Now I know." His eyes twinkled. "Please let me join in. It's probably every man's fantasy to join in private female games."

Ana shook her head. "This is a game you can't play, Tighe. But I'm going upstairs to bed, so you can sit here and try to convince River that you're just as much fun as I am."

"I don't think I can convince her of that," Tighe said. "Give me the game rules so she doesn't beat me."

River and Ana giggled. "Keep my secret," Ana said to River as she got up from the sofa, and River said, "By all means, it's just too much fun to watch men stew in their own juice," and Tighe said, "Hey, you girls can't hog the playbook."

"Yes, we can," Ana said, and went upstairs to think about what she could wear to the elegant Christmas masquerade ball next weekend—if she could get up the courage to watch another woman "win" Dante.

Not a merry occasion at all.

Chapter Eleven

"I'm going with you," Jace said, climbing in beside Dante as he started his truck not five minutes after he and Ana had said goodbye. Her return to Rancho Diablo still had him poleaxed. Never had he been so glad to see someone—and yet, so destroyed.

"I think I know where you're going, and you'll probably need me," Jace said. "Hey, Earth to Dante? Whatever you're thinking about, your brain's puffing smoke out your ears."

"Fine. You can come with me. Keep your thigh-slapping observations to yourself." Dante pulled on his gloves. Snow had begun falling, blanketing the ground in white lushness.

"I'm coming along for the ride," Galen said, opening the door and hopping into the back. "All for one and one for all, as they say."

"We're the Three Musketeers now?" Dante said, grousing slightly. "Hurry, before Ash comes. I don't need the whole gang on this minimission."

"Ash won't be attending. She's too busy making goo-goo eyes at Xav," Jace said. "And don't look for Tighe, either. I saw him slinking off to River's, much good may it do him. One thing I know," Jace said, "is that my brothers have turned into sad little mice who skitter toward a woman like she's a piece of cheese."

"Not me," said Dante, and Galen laughed.

"You're the worst by far. Only Jace and I are managing to hold out, " Galen said. "And frankly I did think Jace was going to manage to pick off River or Ana."

"Nah," Jace said, "they're just my sisters in crime."

Dante frowned. "Crime?" It would have been a crime indeed if Ana had fallen for Jace. Of course, she hadn't fallen for Dante, either, so that was cold comfort. Dante headed down the winding lane toward the main road, turning on the defroster as the truck window fogged from the cold meeting his brothers' hot air.

"Never mind," Jace said, and Galen laughed, clearly knowing exactly what Jace was babbling about. "Just know that the ladies love a man who is true to himself."

"Thank you for that sweet nothing." Dante parked in Storm's drive. "Right now, I want you to be untrue to yourself by not being annoying when we talk to Storm. I need details about his new purchase."

"Is it just killing you that the land we thought we were competing for is Storm's?" Jace got out of the truck, slammed the door.

"No," Dante said, "because I figured Aunt Fiona was setting us up to start with."

"She could have been," Galen said. "But it seems unlikely. Fiona got her other set of nephews married off, but she still played fair. They got land, but more importantly, they've got families they adore. Maybe that's the point."

It didn't matter anymore. Ana didn't seem like she thought of him in any way that portended marriage. Ever since she'd tried on the gown, she'd kept an arm's length away from him, or more.

Except for the night she'd let him make love to her.

But then she'd left.

It was enough to drive a man crazy. "Let's not talk about women, they're a pain in the butt," Dante said. Just then the door was opened by a gorgeous redhead, and he had to work hard not to stare. Beside him, Galen and Jace had gone still and silent—a first.

"Hi," she said, and Dante said, "Hello. We're the Callahans from the ranch over. We'd like to see Storm."

She smiled at all three of them, and Dante thought there was a reason men fancied redheads. Slender and athletic, and with cute freckles across a tiny nose, big blue eyes twinkling at them, Dante thought he and his brothers probably looked like The Three Stooges as they gawked.

"I'm so sorry, but Uncle's not in. I'll tell him you came by."

Dante nodded. "Thank you." He backed off the porch, his shell-shocked brothers following him silently. They got into the truck and Dante watched as the redhead closed the front door. The porch lights threw a glow onto the snow blanketing the house and Dante blew on his hands, wondering when his brothers were going to find their tongues and ask him why he hadn't left a stern message for her to deliver to her uncle.

"That was certainly a surprise," Dante said.

"Yeah," Jace said. "I know you think women are a pain in the butt, yet it didn't look like your butt was hurting you just then, Dante. I know mine wasn't. I was concentrating on a part of me that suddenly felt *good*." He sighed dramatically. "I didn't know angels had hair like fire," Jace said, waxing poetic and annoying.

"I didn't know Storm knew any angels," Galen said.

"When she said he was her uncle, all I could think was lucky son of a—"

"You guys are fogging up the windows again," Dante said. "We're never going to get home unless you quit breathing so hard. You act like you've never seen a woman."

"Not one like that," Jace said.

"Definitely not," Galen agreed. "Wish you'd asked her name."

"Or her marital status, boyfriend status, anything," Jace said.

"Pardon me for not inquiring after her bra size, what side of the bed she prefers and whether she'd ever be interested in going out with a pair of my slow-witted brothers." Dante drummed his fingers on the steering wheel as he drove. "I don't like it. The whole thing smells."

"Why?" Galen asked.

Dante headed down the road toward Rancho Diablo. "I don't get the reasoning behind tying Xav and Ash up."

"All these attacks are designed to run us off the ranch," Galen said. "Scare us, bring us down. Break up the family, make us look over our shoulder constantly. They want the land, the oil wells, the rumored silver mine that the town's been gossiping about for years, and the fabled Diablo mustangs no one's ever seen but us. You think Storm was behind the attempted kidnapping? Is that why we're here?"

"Xav said seven guys jumped them." Dante's uneasiness grew. "They have to be Wolf's men. But Storm bought the land north of us across the canyons, so now we're surrounded on two sides. The bad guys had to have crossed over Storm's land. He should have lookouts. Remember that he was worried about people camping on his land not that long ago."

"Yeah." Galen pondered that. "Whatever you decide, man, we're with you."

"Whatever I decide?" Dante glanced at his brother.

"You're the one with the clarity right now. You seem to be working on a theory," Galen said.

"It isn't coming together," Dante said. "It's right there but I can't see all of it."

"All I can see are those sweet lips on that redhead," Jace enthused from the backseat. "Sweet as a strawberry."

"She bothered me," Dante said. "There was something I just couldn't put my finger on about that lady." Maybe it had been the beautiful face, or the fact that she was related to Storm, whom he trusted about as far as he could throw him.

"I don't know. Suspicion clouds the mind," Jace said. "You've just been really ornery ever since Ana turned you down flat."

Dante's lips creased for a moment. "And how do you know she turned me down flat?"

"Everyone knows," Galen said. "You went around like a bear for weeks after she left. You were telegraphing like crazy. Now she's back and you act like you don't want to talk to her. If I was Ana, I'd be mad."

"Mad?" Dante pulled into the yard, switched off the truck. "About what?"

"You're the one with the clarity these days. Figure it out." Jace slapped him on the back. "Good luck, bro."

"Don't forget the meeting, sunshine," Galen said, shutting the truck door.

Dante had nothing else to say to the two wisenheimers. Maybe he was a little crusty these days, but they weren't shining examples of personality, either, so he didn't care.

They were right about one thing: Ana *had* turned him down flat.

"I hope they both fall for women who understand the thrill of the chase and give my boneheaded brothers a good long slippery one, where there's lots of crow to be eaten at every bend in the road," he muttered, and the winter wind carried his words to the dark velvet skies as he walked into the house.

ALL MEETINGS THAT WERE serious and private were held in the upstairs library of the seven-chimneyed house. Besides Fiona's kitchen, this was Dante's favorite part of the enormous, Tudor-style house that Jeremiah Callahan had built. Jeremiah's dream home, according to Burke, who labeled himself something of a historian on the house and its grounds. The place was very comfortable, despite its enormous size, and Dante felt instinctively that Jeremiah and Molly would never have left it, nor, more important, deserted their six sons, unless the danger had been extreme.

His own parents, Carlos and Julia, had followed in Jeremiah's and Molly's footsteps. Fighting the good fight was in their blood. Dante knew all the Callahans came by their instinct to protect their own from those who had gone before. Running Bear had spent years trying to keep his family safe—how heartbreaking it must be that the evil chasing the Callahans was overseen by Running Bear's own son, Wolf, on behalf of the cartel. His brothers, Jeremiah and Carlos, had been warriors, yet Wolf had gone over to the bad side. How did that happen in families?

Dante appropriated a leather chair for himself and

waited for Galen to begin the meeting. His mind drifted to Ana. Had she come back because of the children? She wasn't taking her old job back, and she was leaving after Christmas. This had his radar up as much as anything. Why would she come back here for the holidays?

He gazed at the many windows of the library, darkened by the night, admiring the electric candles Fiona had set in every window and the beribboned wreaths hanging above them. When he and his siblings had grown up in the tribe, they'd celebrated the holidays differently. He liked this way, too. But sometimes he was homesick. None of them could ever go home again, because Running Bear had set them on a mission to keep Carlos and Julia, and Jeremiah and Molly, safe. There could be no tracks to the past.

He understood family and the longing for home. But Ana had returned and, frankly, his holiday season would be a bit brighter because of it.

It would be even better if she'd show up in his bed again, with a little Christmas surprise for him. He sighed, lost in the fantasy, until Galen cleared his throat loudly. His brothers and sister stared at him in astonishment.

"What?" Dante asked.

"Brother, you muttered something," Ash said, "which sounded distinctly like 'Christmas kisses.'"

"I thought he said, 'Ana kisses,'" Jace said, shaking his head.

"I just thought he was drooling." Tighe peered at him. "Hello? You okay in there?"

"I'm fine," Dante said. "I didn't say anything. Or drool." He'd been lost in a lusty fantasy, certainly, but he'd been keeping those under his hat for months. "Proceed with the meeting."

"You sure?" Galen hesitated. "Because if you're not feeling well, if you have things you need to attend to—"

"I don't." Dante felt himself becoming grouchier by the second. "You guys all have such vivid imaginations."

Ash laid her head against his shoulder. "Leave him alone. He's allowed to hallucinate on occasion."

Galen shook his head. "All right, the first topic—"

"Excuse me," Burke said, entering the room. "I hate to disturb the meeting, but the new bodyguard is downstairs."

"Can't it wait until after?" Galen asked. "It's like catching birds to get all this crew assembled and paying attention."

"Ms. Kendall said Sloan told her that the new bodyguard was to be introduced immediately, so there were no new faces at the ranch that no one recognized," Burke said.

"That's right," Sloan said, rising to his feet. "It'll only take a second. We can't afford to have anybody on the ranch that we don't know, and I want to make certain Kendall engaged a bodyguard that we're all happy with. Including my boys and River."

Dante thought that was wise. They couldn't be too cautious. They filed down the stairs, grouping into the family room.

"This is Miss Sawyer Cash," Burke said, slipping from the room.

Dante stared at the gorgeous redheaded bombshell standing next to Kendall, who gazed around at everyone with a delighted smiled on her face. "Guys, I'd like you to meet the new bodyguard for the twins.

Sawyer, these are the Callahans. I'll let them introduce themselves."

"Won't be necessary for me," Dante said, but before
he could say *we've already met and I don't like this,*
Jace stumbled forward, pushing Galen out of his way.

"How do you do?" he said to the woman they'd met
just thirty minutes ago on Storm Cash's porch. Uncle
Storm's niece was going to be living on Rancho Diablo, privy to Callahan secrets and precious children?

Dante backed away. Nothing good could come of
this. Not one thing, especially if his brothers were
thinking with something other than their pea-size
brains.

Chapter Twelve

The next day dawned colder than ever, and Ana decided the only way to warm up was to go help Fiona string Christmas lights over the corral rails. She loved days like this at Rancho Diablo, when the ranch was wrapped in a cozy blanket of white twinkling snow.

Fiona smiled as Ana came to join her. "Good morning! You're up early! Did you sleep well?"

"Like a baby. And speaking of babies, the boys sleep through the night now, like angels. They're growing so fast." Ana felt a little wistful about everything she was going to miss as the boys grew into young men.

"Children do grow up fast." Fiona smiled at her. "You're coming to the Christmas ball, aren't you? I simply won't allow you to say no! The decorations my committee have begun putting up are simply fabulous this year!"

Ana smiled at Fiona's enthusiasm. "Of course I'll be there. I wouldn't miss it for the world."

"Good." Fiona handed her a roll of white lights. "Twine those over the rails. Burke will come by later and put the whole thing together. If I tried to manage the electrical, I'd have this place wired for disaster." She got out some wreaths and began situating them along the fence. "This year I plan to outdo myself. I hope you brought a lovely gown for the party!" Stopping, she turned to look at Ana. "Oh, I'm so sorry. You probably don't want to talk about beautiful gowns."

"It's fine." Ana didn't like to think about the one that had not been "magic" on her, but that was over now, in the past. "I won't be wearing fancy dress to the masquerade ball, Fiona. I hope you don't mind."

"I'd figured as much," Fiona said. "We didn't give you much time to prepare. It can be difficult to find the just-right outfit!"

Dante walked up, handed Fiona and Ana both a cup of hot cocoa. "Good morning, ladies."

"Hi." Ana felt breathless in Dante's presence. He smiled at her and her heart melted despite the cold. She loved his smile and his dark hair and the way she always felt happy when he was around.

"Hi," he said. "Want to ride into town?"

Ana blinked. "Sure. Where are we going?"

"It's a surprise." He glanced at Fiona. "Do you mind if I borrow her?"

"Not a bit," Fiona said cheerfully. "Thanks for the cocoa, favored nephew, though please don't tell your brothers I identify you as such."

He kissed her cheek. "All your secrets are safe with me, Aunt."

She rapped him with a decorative candy cane and then tucked it into the corral lights. "I have no secrets. I'm an open book. Speaking of books, I tap you to read 'The Night Before Christmas' to the little ones on Christmas Eve."

"Be happy to." Dante tipped his hat and nodded to Ana to go with him.

Ana followed Dante to his truck, and he opened the door for her and said, "I was hoping I'd run in to you."

She waited until he got in the truck and started it. "You know where I'm staying if something's on your mind."

"I didn't know anything was on my mind, exactly, until I met Sawyer last night." He glanced at her, then steered the truck down to the main road. "What did you think of her?"

"It's not my business to think anything," Ana hedged. "Kendall hired her, and she's experienced with hiring people all around the world. Sawyer must have the qualifications Kendall wants."

"I just don't like it." Dante shook his head. "There's just something fundamentally wrong to my mind in having our neighbor's niece working for us."

"Maybe you could mention your concerns to Kendall."

"For now, I'll just ask you to keep an eye on her, if you don't mind."

Ana blinked. "Dante, I don't want to. I'm training her to take my position. I don't want to think anything of her except for her capabilities. It's my job to protect the little boys, not to dissect the new girl." She shook her head. "I trust Kendall's judgment."

He nodded. "You're right. I shouldn't have asked. I didn't realize how awkward it would be for you."

"Why do you dislike Storm so much?"

"Just seems like when funky things happen, he's not far away. Maybe I'm just normally suspicious. I don't know." Dante shrugged. "I talked to Sheriff Cartwright in town, and one thing he mentioned is that Storm's been dating Lulu Feinstrom in town. Maybe he's too busy to cause trouble."

"I love Lulu's blackberry pies. And she makes the best watermelon daiquiris."

"Yes, she's a nice lady."

"But you've always relied on hunches," Ana said.

"I believe in the power of intuition."

She did, too. "Maybe you could talk to Kendall. Ask her if she knew that Sawyer was Storm's niece when she hired her."

"She had to. Moreover, Sloan had to be on board."

That was true. Still, Dante's unease made Ana uncomfortable, because of the twins. "Kendall wouldn't hire anyone who would endanger the boys."

"I know. Forget I said anything. Let's concentrate on things we can control. Like Fiona's shindig. You're coming, right?"

She nodded. "I'm looking forward to supporting Fiona's ball. And I wish you the best of luck as the main course."

"Yeah, well. Anything for charity." They pulled in front of the bridal gown shop and Dante parked the truck. "If I take you in here with me, will you burst into flame one foot past the door?"

She looked at him. "I hope not. Have you heard rumors to the contrary?"

"Just checking."

She got out and followed him. "Are you cross-dressing to play your part for the masquerade ball?"

He shook his head. "Fiona thought you might need a dress. This is the place for costume ball glory, or so I'm told."

She stopped in her tracks. "I don't need a dress."

He gazed down at her. "Fiona says—"

"Fiona is trying to be nice, and you are, too, but I'm just going to wear a church dress. I'll be fine."

Dante's navy eyes were filled with indecision. "Listen, I don't know so much about ladies and dresses, but it seems like since prehistoric times when humans put on fig leaves, the lady wanted hers to be the prettiest in the forest."

She started to walk back toward the truck. "I appreciate that Fiona has sent you on a mission, but I'm perfectly comfortable with what I've got."

"You've got a mask? We could just pick up a mask—"

"Dante. I'm fine." She'd grab one when he wasn't around. She wished Fiona hadn't sent Dante to do this. "I'm sure you have more important things to do than shop, so why don't we head back?"

"Not so fast. I never come to town without making a stop at the Books'n'Bingo."

"How you don't gain weight, I'll never know." Ana decided she could at least be gracious and humor him on his cookie hunt.

"I don't gain weight because I'm too busy chasing nephews and bad guys, and sometimes my aunt Fiona sends me on wild-goose chases. She underestimated your stubborn side." He stopped, and after a moment, gazed down at her. "Listen, I want you to do something for me. If I give you a couple hundred bucks, will you secretly buy me?"

"At the auction?" She laughed a bit uncomfortably. "Dante, don't ask me. Please." It would be so embarrassing later, when she told him her secret. She didn't want any part of the auction. She planned to attend the ball, and when the charity bit began, she was heading home. "I'm not planning to stay for the auction."

He led her to the teashop. They stood under the bright awning, and as the sun twinkled off the glass windows on the main street, Ana thought her heart was breaking just like glass dropped on the ground.

"Ana, I'm trying to avoid an awkward night with a woman I don't know. You buy me, I'm off the hook. You have no idea how nervous I am about being the grab bag on Saturday night."

"You mean the grand prize." She giggled in spite of the delicacy of the situation. "I thought men liked variety. Change of pace and all that. Fresh game."

He sighed. "We do. When we control it."

"Whoever buys you will be most appreciative, I'm sure."

"You don't understand. I'm picky about women. Some might almost say to a fault." He really did look worried. "What if she laughs too loud? What if she doesn't like country-and-western music? What if she's looking for more than I want to give?"

"Eek," Ana said. "Can we skip details like that?"

"I'm talking about *dessert,*" he said, sounding a bit desperate. "Something past a quick dinner."

She stared at him, trying not to laugh. "I think for a couple hundred bucks, a lady expects more than a peanut butter and jelly sandwich, Dante. At least steak, salad and vegetables, and then some chocolate mouse or chocolate pecan pie."

He looked alarmed. "I could be stuck for three hours with a woman I have nothing in common with, and you could save me by taking my money and buying me."

"That's rigging the game, which is very unfair." Ana shook her head. "There are over a hundred women coming to Diablo for the fun, and you want to sandbag the contest. It's not sporting."

"You'd feel differently if you were the grand prize." He looked positively depressed at the notion. "Never mind. I didn't say that. Don't tell my aunt what I asked you."

"There's an elementary school roof on the line. You have to be a lively grand prize. Don't let your family down." She pushed the door open and walked into the store. "Be brave."

"I don't think you're paying attention." He followed her into the teashop and lowered his voice conspiratorially. "Rumor has it that three women have pooled their funds, and they intend to share me."

"A fate worse than death?" She considered the treats in the pie case. The cupcakes looked fabulous, and the wreath and snowman shaped cookies caught her eye. "Some men would be flattered."

"I'm not. Sheriff Cartwright told me that every bed-and-breakfast in town is booked, and every restaurant has been booked solid with reservations since last week."

"Aren't you happy your aunt is such a trooper for Diablo?" She looked at him curiously. "Just think of all the children who will appreciate your suffering." She patted him on the arm. "I'll take one of those cupcakes with the stars on top, please, Mavis," she said with a smile, and pulled out her wallet.

"I've got it," Dante said gruffly. "We cover all expenses at Rancho Diablo for our bodyguards."

She put her wallet back in her bag. "All right. Thank you."

Mavis smiled at both of them. "It's so good you came in today. We just had our two-hundredth ticket purchased for the auction, Dante!"

He looked at Ana as if to say *help!* "That's wonderful, Mavis."

"It's so lovely that you're back in town. Do you have

a costume, Ana?" Mavis asked kindly, and Corinne came over with a freshly baked tray of cookies to set out.

"All the ladies in town are so excited about their costumes," Corinne told Ana. "Fiona has decided to award prizes for the top three ladies and the guys." She smiled at Dante. "I bet you win."

Ana could practically feel Dante radiating discomfort. "Who chooses the costume winners?"

Nadine came over with a teapot and a grin. "Fiona has decided that three large barrels will be put out for the ladies, and three for the guys. Everyone will drop in a dime for the person they think has the best costume! The fullest barrel wins."

"My aunt's ideas on how to generate funds is boundless."

"I think it's wonderful. Who chooses the initial three finalists?" Ana asked.

"Well, let's see," Mavis said. "We hadn't thought that far. You do it, dear. You're an out-of-towner now, you'll be fairest. Don't you think, ladies?"

Her friends nodded enthusiastically.

"All right," Ana said. "I'd love to help." It would keep her out of the way, keep her from focusing on the ladies chatting up Dante.

They beamed at her. "We knew we could count on you. Though please don't choose this handsome devil just because he's sweet on you," Corinne said, and the ladies went on to helping the next customers in line.

Ana glanced at Dante. He got busy grabbing napkins and some other items from the tea tray and headed over to a table. She followed him, hardly knowing what to say. Dante wasn't sweet on her. He'd not called her once when she was in Buffalo Gap. He hadn't paid her much attention since she'd been back, unless his aunt sent him or they ran into each other by accident.

"Anyway," Ana said, sitting down at the table to join him, "what makes you think a couple hundred bucks will be required to secure your auction? I'll probably have plenty left over."

He glanced up. "You'll do it?"

"I'll rescue you, Dante. I have to take pity on a man who's as awkward around women as you are, I suppose," she teased.

"I'll take you out for a dinner you won't forget," he promised, sounding relieved and grateful, and Ana thought, *Wonderful, because I'm eating for two these days, and we really seem to be fancying sweet stuff.*

Dante might not be sweet on her, but she sure was on him.

Chapter Thirteen

The early hours of the morning of the Christmas ball began with four inches of snow on the ground and a lump of coal in Dante's heart. "That's not right," Dante muttered, peering out his bedroom window. "It's not a lump of coal in my heart. It's probably ice from a certain lady that I can't seem to warm up."

"Must you talk to yourself?" Tighe demanded, meeting him at his bedroom door with a cup of coffee. "Tonight's our big night, bro. We are the stars, the honey to the bees, the big men on campus. It's going to be awesome!"

Dante slurped the coffee, tried to keep up with Tighe's blather. He felt better knowing that Ana would save him tonight. Maybe it was playing dirty pool, but he didn't care. Did he want to be with Ana or a woman he didn't know?

It was simple. Ana. No question.

"I'm looking forward to being the big cheese," Tighe said cheerfully. "I hope the woman that wins me is drop-dead sexy, and smiles a lot, and wants to kiss me all night long."

"I hope she's a hundred years old and wants you to

rub her feet," Dante said sourly. "Not that there's anything wrong with that."

"Yes, there is." Tighe followed him into the kitchen, watching as he popped a slice of coffee cake into the microwave. "How could you say such a thing to your twin? I only wish you the best! Well, not the best, *I* want the best, but you know what I mean. I'll get the most beautiful woman at the ball, and you get the second most beautiful. That's my optimistic outlook."

"That's shallow," Dante pointed out. "Not everything is about looks."

"No," Tighe agreed with a hopeful expression, "it's all about getting naked."

"I hope not." The only woman he wanted to see naked was Ana, but it seemed those days were past.

"I heard," Tighe said as the microwave dinged, "that ten women have pooled their resources so they can bid on me. Ten ladies, all to myself." He sighed with joy. "Sheer heaven."

Dante sighed and sat down to shovel the coffee cake before he ran late for chores. "Listen, you can have whoever buys me—unless it's Ana," he said, the stroke of genius hitting him belatedly. "Or someone else I know and could stand taking out for an evening. Like our sister." Maybe Ashlyn would take pity on him if Ana decided not to help him. There was no telling with women.

"You've really got a thing for Ana, don't you?" Tighe looked at him curiously. "Have you ever considered just telling her?"

"Have you told River about your thing?"

"No, but she seems to be otherwise attached. Ana's not, as far as we know. I guess there could be someone back in Gopher Gap—"

"Buffalo Gap," Dante said. He pushed the coffee cake away, not wanting to think about Ana having "somebody" back home. "How much did the victim go for at the last auction?"

Tighe looked at him. "I have no idea. Why are you so worried? You should be thrilled to be the object of desire. It may be the only time in your life that you'll be a rock star, bro."

"I just don't need that much ego stroke." He looked at his brother. "I award whoever wins me to you— unless it's someone we know."

"Can't do it. Wouldn't be fair to Fiona," Tighe said, suddenly turning purist. "She'd get in all kinds of doo for false advertising, and that would hamper any future auctions. We just can't let that happen. It affects too many people. Can't you just relax and enjoy being hunk o' the holidays?"

"Not exactly. Never mind." Dante headed to the barns. He hoped Ana wouldn't change her mind about saving him. He'd given her two hundred bucks with which to bid and offered her a dinner. Maybe he should have thrown in an additional incentive.

Thing was, she really didn't seem to want anything from him.

She *couldn't* let him down.

"Hi, cowboy," he heard, and Dante turned.

"Hello," he said to the tiny brunette standing in the barn. If his mind weren't so stuck on Ana, he probably would have called this tiny doll adorable. "Can I help you?"

"Oh, yes," she said with a smile. "I just came by to sample the goods before I bid."

She wrapped her arms around his neck and gave him the smooch of a lifetime, shocking him so badly his poor stupid brain short-circuited before he pulled away. "Wow," he said, "uh, thank you, little lady, I guess, but if you don't mind, I'd appreciate not being sampled."

Her dark green eyes glowed. "See you tonight, cowboy."

She sauntered out of the barn. Dante ripped off his hat, then his bandana, and wiped his mouth. Holy smoke! He'd be in a real pickle if that woman tried to win him. He'd never get Ana to slow down enough to catch her.

He pulled out his cell phone and dialed. He heard a bunch of muffled murmuring. "Hello? Tighe?"

"Yeah," his brother finally said.

"Listen, there's a stray brunette on the property heading your way. Could you escort her off the ranch and let her know that those no-trespassing signs are there for a reason?"

"Sure," he said, and then his phone clicked off.

Ana tapped his arm, startling him so badly he nearly jumped out of his boots. "Where'd you come from?"

"Right there," Ana said. "Fiona sent me to the barn to freshen the coffee and check out the fridge for the ranch hands."

"Oh." He hoped he'd wiped all the lipstick off.

She gazed at him. "I think that lady might be a rather eager bidder tonight."

Busted. He pulled a couple more hundred bucks from his wallet and handed it to her. "I'm counting on you."

Tighe came strolling into the barn, whistling. "That little brunette was quite the jalapeno. If she's the quality we can expect to bid tonight, we're in fine shape. I barely pulled her off my face."

"That's funny," Ana said, "because Dante had trouble pulling her off of his, too."

"She was sampling," Dante said, and Ana laughed.

"Obviously. Bye, Tighe." She left the barn and Dante stared after her.

"She saw you kissing another woman?" Tighe asked. "Not smooth, dude."

"Thanks. Like I didn't know." He sighed. "I have a bad feeling about tonight. Really bad."

"Well," Tighe said cheerfully, "I, for one, am as excited as a little kid on Christmas."

"I think I was safer on Firefreak back in the day," Dante said, and went to take his mind off Ana, if he could.

But after tonight, after the auction was over, he was going to turn the tables on his bad luck. He was running out of time, and even if Ana St. John didn't think too highly of him at the moment, he was determined to show her he was the man she wanted.

It wouldn't be easy. At the moment he was pretty low in her estimation—but surely there was no place to go but up.

Two hours before the ball, Ana marched to her closet, stared inside at the clothes she'd brought with her. Stretchy pants, some loose blouses and sweaters, a black skirt long enough to wear with boots.

All right. That's what she was going to wear. She pulled on the skirt, put on the boots, tugged a red sweater over her head. At least she'd be warm, because tonight was certain to be even colder than it was now. She told herself she'd be a lot more comfortable than the ladies in evening gowns because they'd be freezing.

It wasn't a sexy ensemble, and she wished she

hadn't seen that darling little brunette wrapped around Dante's strong body. She wasn't jealous, because she'd heard everything—knew that Dante hadn't been too happy about being caught off guard—but at the same time she was jealous because she knew that one day, some beautiful woman would figure out a way to drag him to an altar.

As handsome princes went, Dante was a stud. The women were going to go nuts tonight.

River came into her room. "I brought you something." She handed her a pretty black sequined mask, then glanced down at Ana's outfit. "Is that what you're wearing?"

"Casual, huh?"

"I like it. You'll be warm." River gave her a quick hug. "To thine own self be true, I always say."

"Yes, well, look out for a man-hungry little brunette tonight when the bidding begins. You've got competition."

River looked slightly worried. "Is she pretty?"

"Yes." Ana nodded. "Are you ever going to tell Tighe how you feel?"

"No way. He'd run off like a rabbit."

"You never know." Ana smoothed her skirt, then began putting her hair up.

River sat on the bed. "Speaking of confessing things, I really thought you would have told Dante about the baby by now. How do you keep that secret to yourself?"

"Something told me it was better to wait until after Christmas."

River nodded. "I'm sure you're right. How do you feel?"

"Like the luckiest woman in the world. I can't wait

to be a mother." Ana smiled at River in the mirror. "Pregnancy is really the most magical thing."

River got up. "I'm so happy for you. By the way, I heard you're the secret first round judge on costumes. I just want you to know that my dress is a knockout. Feel free to admire it and place me in the final round if you wish. I've always wanted to see my name on a large barrel."

She giggled, and Ana smiled. "I won't know it's you since you'll be wearing a mask. Thank you for mine, though I think most people will figure out that I'm the out-of-towner who doesn't have a fancy gown from the Diablo bridal shop."

"You'll be stunning. This is going to be such a wonderful night," River said. "I'm going to catch my cowboy tonight!"

She practically waltzed out of the room. Shaking her head, Ana chose a lipstick but then put it back. She pondered her image, thought about the pretty brunette kissing Dante—even though he'd clearly been unhappy about it. "Maybe a different blouse," she murmured, studying herself. She looked as if she was going to a luncheon, not a ball.

Who was she kidding? She wanted to be beautiful for Dante. She dreamed of him taking her in his arms and kissing her again, making love to her.

"Why was I so stubborn about a dress?" she muttered. "I shouldn't have been such a spoilsport. That's what I get for guarding my emotions." She cro
to her closet and pulled open the door, gas
magic wedding dress hanging there in al'
chantment, twinkling and beautiful, be
beguiling. Sexy gold pumps and an elega
shone beside the splendid dress.

"Oh, thank you!" Ana exclaimed, and if she had a fairy godmother who was listening with a fond smile, Ana dearly hoped she knew how grateful she was to put this lovely gown on one more time. It was perfect for tonight.

She stepped into the dress, pulling it up slowly, the beauty of it wrapping her in romance. Touching the skirt with wonder, Ana admired the gown in the mirror with misty tears of delight in her eyes. Dante walked into the room wearing his tux, the most handsome man she'd ever seen, smiling at her in the reflection, and Ana whirled around. "Dante! Isn't this the most lovely gown you've ever seen?"

But he wasn't there. She was alone.

Yet Dante *had* been there, and they'd smiled at each other. She'd felt his kindness, his gentleness and maybe even—dared she hope?—his love for her.

Ana turned back to look in the mirror. The gown twinkled and sparkled, its long skirt resplendent with glints of ruby and gold.

Maybe tonight would be the most magical night of her life.

Chapter Fourteen

Dante felt calm as over a hundred women eagerly grouped close to the stage in the theater room of the Diablo library, squealing and ready to bid as his twin went on the block. Normally the enormous room was the setting for puppet shows and the yearly *Nutcracker* rendition. Ballet recitals and musicals were also held here. Years ago, it had been determined that the library would be a first-class theater for gatherings, and he'd be willing to bet that Diablo's great hall and stage had much to thank the town mothers for as far as planning.

One of those town mothers thought nothing of auctioning off her own nephews for charity, but the best part of that was that he'd outthought his wiry aunt. Ana owed him. He'd saved her, now it was her turn to bring the cavalry.

He watched Tighe doing his Studly-do-right act across the stage, to the delight of the ladies, who had their paddles ready. Some of the eager bidders used their paddles to fan themselves as Tighe strutted his stuff in the best rendition of a Chippendales dancer, priming the pump as everyone waited for the emcee— Fiona—to start the bidding. Dante shook his head embarrassing," he muttered, and his sister cocked her head as she watched Tighe perform.

"The ladies seem to be eating it up," Ash observed. "But they're going to go for you, too. You look like Zorro."

He smirked, feeling very well protected behind his mask. Ash looked very cute in hers, he had to admit, and somewhere in this excited crowd Ana no doubt lurked, waiting to set him free.

Fiona took the stage, turned on a microphone so she could be heard over the thumping music and the squeals and applause of the ladies. "We'll start the bidding at twenty-five dollars!" she exclaimed. "Do I hear twenty-five dollars for the new roof for the elementary school?

"You should bid to help him out," Dante said, watching his twin flex his muscles. "He's not going to go for more than a hundred, tops." He felt pretty smug that he'd given Ana four hundred to cover his own purchase.

"I'm not raising his bid," Ash said. "He's going to do fine."

"I'll bid two thousand!" came a voice from the back, and the room almost went silent as everyone turned to stare at the bidder.

Of course the mystery woman could only be identified by the number on her paddle she waved gaily, but Dante knew who she was despite her mask. "That's the new bodyguard! Storm's niece, Sawyer!"

"Yeah. Guess Sawyer thinks she'll like kissing Tighe better than you," Ash observed drily.

"Two thousand it is!" Fiona called, clearly delighted. "Do I heard twenty-one?" She glanced around the room. "Dante, come up here and join your twin on stage! I promised these ladies a double dose and I don't want anybody going home disappointed!"

"Oh, no," Dante said, and Ash burst out laughing.

"Go on, Grand Prize. Do your thing. Bring home the bacon for Diablo!"

Fiona waved wildly at him, and Dante knew he was stuck. He wasn't prepared for this. Nowhere did he see Ana's shiny golden hair. Beside the staircase leading to the stage was a gorgeous fairy-tale princess, her domino in place, hair piled high, wearing a fire-engine red gown. But he barely had time to register anything else as his brother pulled him onto the stage, starting his butt-shaking routine again.

The ladies went nuts. "I'm not dancing around like I've got ants in my pants," Dante said, and Tighe pretended like he was pulling off his bow tie—no, wait, he was pulling off his tie, very slowly, very suggestively—and then he tossed it into the sea of delighted women.

"Try to act lively," Tighe told him. "You had more action going when you were getting stomped by Firefreak." He danced by, unbuttoned a few buttons on the top of his tux shirt, electrifying the room.

"Twenty-five!" a lady yelled.

"Remember, you're just bidding for Tighe," Fiona said, "the grand prize comes later! Dante, show the ladies why you're the grand prize!"

"Holy smokes," he said, as the spotlight turned fullbore on him. Tighe danced around him, hogging the attention, laughing at his brother.

"You've sure got a stick up your—"

"Never mind," Dante said, "you're not the only one who knows how to show off. But I'm the grand prize because I come later." He walked back down the stairs, and the ladies grabbed at him, but he said, "The best things in life are worth waiting for," and went to Ash for protection.

"Chicken," Ash said. "I think you should have at least doffed your shirt for these women."

"I can't." He glanced around for Ana. She'd said she'd be wearing a simple skirt and blouse as she hadn't brought any party clothes with her—and she'd refused his offer to get her something pretty. "I can't raise their hopes and then give them nothing."

"Hey, Grand Prize, you're going to give them something tonight," Ash said. "That's what Grand Prizes do. Whatever Tighe does, you're going to have to do better."

"Trust me," Fiona announced, "tonight I have five of Diablo's best for you to bid on, but these Callahan twins are worth every penny of your donations to the elementary school roof!"

"Twenty-six!" Storm's niece called.

"If she's the new bodyguard, does it seem like a conflict of interest for her to spend so much money on our dolt of a brother?" Ash asked.

"There are no real rules in Diablo. Fiona makes 'em and she breaks 'em. And if the lady wants to spend her money on our blockheaded brother, Fiona will wrap Tighe in a bow and give him out."

"You know that's twenty-six hundred she's bidding," Ash said, "as in getting close to three grand. How much did you give Ana to bid on you?"

"Four hundred," Dante said, and then he stopped. "How do you know about that?"

"Because Ana told me." Ash winked at him. "I'm supposed to keep it a dire secret, which I will, but unless you're the dud of the night, your paltry few Benjamins aren't going to save you."

Ash was right. "I don't see Ana anywhere," he said, desperately glancing around for her.

"Maybe she decided she didn't want to be responsible for saving you." Ash shrugged, laughing at Tighe as he pretended to undo his zipper, throwing the crowd of females into a frenzy. "You know, I never really thought about it before, but you and Tighe are really only twins in appearance."

"What does that mean?" He scanned the crowd for Ana, beginning to fear that his sister was right: she wasn't here.

"Tighe's more free-spirited than you are." Ash glanced up at him. "You're not exactly Mr. Excitement."

"Really? I feel like my life is pretty much out of control," Dante said. "I feel as if I'm living on the edge."

She smiled. "You used to be a wild man. Seems like you've settled down since you came back to Diablo. Maybe being on the rodeo circuit tamed you a bit."

He shook his head. "If I'm tamer, it wasn't rodeo that did it." It was Ana, but he wasn't sharing. Truth was, he wasn't looking forward to preening like a peacock in front of a bunch of manhunting women. He'd hoped Ana would hunt him—but by the look of things, she wasn't going to be flashing a paddle for him.

"Sold for twenty-eight hundred dollars!" Fiona exclaimed. "A Diablo record!"

Tighe jumped off the stage and scooped Storm's niece up into his arms. Some ladies laughed and some sighed enviously, but all Dante knew was that the only arms he wanted to jump into tonight were Ana's.

ANA WAS IN A BIT OF A PANIC. She was supposed to be picking six finalists for the costume judging—but she could barely keep her attention from what was happening on stage. Watching Tighe leer and jump around astonished her—but when Dante got on stage, energizing the ladies, Ana's heart had sunk. It was all in good fun, but at the same time, she didn't fancy the idea of knowing that some woman was going to throw herself at Dante.

Actually, a lot of women.

It was hard to judge costumes with an impartial eye knowing that the most beautifully dressed woman might be the one who won Dante.

"Hi," someone said, and Ana turned to find Ash laughing at her.

"Hi, yourself. Even with your mask, I know it's you because of that silvery hair of yours." Ana glanced around the room. "Pick out three men and three women to be the finalists for Best Costume. I can't be impartial."

Ash laughed. "You win flat-out for Most Beautiful." She gazed at Ana's gown. "How did you get the magic wedding dress to change colors?"

"How did you know it was the magic wedding dress? And how did you know it was me?" Ana asked.

"Anyone can see the magic, if they just look," Ash said. "I've seen this magic many times before."

"Oh. Right," Ana said, not understanding but not surprised by Ash's words.

"And I knew it was you because you were the last one to try on the gown. It's gorgeous," Ash said. "I never imagined it could change colors."

"I don't know why it did. It was this way the first time I tried it on," Ana said, and Ash nodded.

"Clearly, this is you," she said. "The gown reflects

the wearer. So you must be…" She looked at Ana. "The only thing that comes to mind is red-hot."

Ana laughed. "The red-hot bodyguard. Yes, I chose to be a bodyguard because I had such a cooking personality. Get me near a fire and the fire blows itself out because I'm so smokin'."

Ash shook her head. "Not like that, silly. It's your past, your experiences that shaped you. Are you hiding a red-hot facet of your personality? A secret that would shock everyone?"

Ana shook her head. "Not really. I think I'm just a plain Jane." Was pregnancy a red-hot secret? She didn't think so.

"Anyway," Ash said cheerfully, "I choose you to be a finalist. There's not a gown here that touches that one."

"Thank you, but that wouldn't be fair. A judge can't choose herself."

Ana glanced over at the second offering for the night, a tall cowboy with short brown hair and big brown eyes. Dante was nowhere to be seen, and Tighe was swallowed up by a gaggle of women as energetic music played over the speakers. "Ash, you pick the six finalists. I'm going home."

"Home!" Ash stared at her. "You can't! You promised my brother you'd rescue him!"

"With four hundred bucks?" Ana shook her head. "Dante is grand prize. Fiona clearly intends to rake in all she can tonight. Four hundred dollars would only be a token effort. Dante's on his own."

"You can't say that! He's—well, he's counting on you," Ash said. "I've got ten dollars in my purse."

"That'll help," Ana said. "Thank you, but I don't think it'll kill Dante to be won by an eager woman."

"It might," Ash said. "I know. Let's go through the audience and spread a rumor that the grand prize is a dud."

Ana gasped. "You wouldn't do that to your brother!"

"He'd thank me." Ashlyn shrugged.

"Your aunt wouldn't! She's trying to get a new roof for the elementary school. She's counting on Dante to bring in lots of money!"

"This is true," Ash said, "but it wouldn't be wholly bad if the tables got turned on the good aunt for once."

"No," Ana said decisively. "Don't you dare rig your aunt's charity ball. You should be supporting her, Ash. If anything, you should go out there and spread a rumor that Dante is the most amazing brother on the planet, a handsome prince like no other!"

Ash stared at her. "Could you just spend one second being selfish? You know, a little manipulation goes a long way."

"Maybe, but cheaters never win. I honestly believe that."

"Are you determined to win my brother?" Ash asked, looking at her intently.

"I— Not determined," Ana said. "*Hopeful* is the word I would have chosen. If it's meant to be."

"Maybe things are meant to be," Ash said doggedly. "Maybe some things happen because they get helped along. Witness the wily aunt. She's always helping something."

Squeals went up as the second bachelor's bidding went over a thousand dollars. She really didn't think she could bear to watch man-wild women bid on Dante. "I can't do it," Ana said. "No cheating."

"So bid on Dante yourself."

Ana shook her head. "I'm not spending three or four grand I don't have!"

Ashlyn smiled. "Not even to keep other ladies away from the father of your child?"

"It just doesn't seem right," Ana began, and then she realized Ash's eyes were twinkling. "I didn't say anything about a child, Ashlyn."

"You didn't have to," Ash said, linking her arm through Ana's. "The dress tells the story. I knew you must be hiding a red-hot secret!" She laughed, delighted. "You're going to be my sister-in-law!"

"I don't know that. And you can't tell Dante," Ana said, a bit desperately. "Promise me you won't say a word, Ashlyn. I'm not telling him until after Christmas!"

"Not a word will pass my lips. Come on, let's go turn in your finalists."

"You're not going to encourage me anymore to bid on your brother?"

"Nope," Ash said, "my brother deserves to be auctioned off to a toothless witchy-poo for getting you in the family way. And I hope that's what happens! Let's see if we can find one," she said, glancing around the crowd. "Let's see if we can find an out-of-towner who looks like she might be bossy as heck and smell of mothballs, and be pushing the dark side of eighty."

"Ashlyn Callahan!" Ana was shocked.

"Dante was clearly just too lazy to drive to the drugstore. Or you wouldn't be in the mess you're in."

"That's not true," Ana said. "We did use a condom. And I'm not in a mess."

"Condoms he's had in his wallet for two years don't count." She sighed. "Honestly, sometimes I worry about my brothers."

Ana glanced around at the crush of women. "Help me pick some finalists, please."

"I suppose we should select out-of-towners to give them the most bang for their buck. Paying nearly three grand for my brother is egregious."

Ana smiled. "Okay. You pick the ladies, I'll choose the men."

"All right. That's easy." Ash glanced around the room. "Choose blue gown over there, paddle number ninety-eight. I like the feathers in her hair. That Cinderella over there deserves a nod just for the fact that I bet her feet are killing her in those pumps. I hope those aren't really glass."

"The gown is lovely," Ana agreed. "And how about that wonderful dress with the roses all over it? I bet she sewed those on herself."

"It's eye-stopping," Ash said. "Mine are certainly stopped. I can't look away."

Ana couldn't, either. To her astonishment, Dante neared the steps, about to walk up onto the stage, and stopped when the little rose gown jumped into his arms. Ana recognized her as the tiny brunette who'd kissed Dante in the barn.

"Oh, wow," Ash said, "scratch her off the finalists list."

"Exactly," Ana said.

"Let me have that stupid list," Ash said, taking it from Ana's hand. She wrote down two numbers—the blue gown and the Cinderella gown, and then she wrote Ana's name. "There are your finalists. You can take off your name, but I advise you not to hide your light under a basket. As you can see, the race around here goes to the swiftest."

"I don't want to be in a race. Dante either wants to

be with me or he doesn't. And I am counting on you not to say anything to your brother." She stared Ash down. "I'll be fine no matter what happens. I've been blessed with a baby. That's such a miracle I just know everything else will work out, too."

"I'll go turn your list in, Miss Modest." Ash went off with the list of female finalists, and Ana watched Dante set the rose gown on her feet gently, avoiding her as she tried to sneak a kiss from him.

Okay, so he was man candy. Ana went to turn in her three names for male costume finalists—choosing Jace, Tighe and Dante, because they were all crazy-handsome. "Mavis, here's the guys' list. Where's the list of female finalists?"

"Right there." Mavis pointed to a piece of paper lying on the table as she grabbed a few Magic Markers to make signs for the barrels. "I'm just going to check these numbers you gave me against registered names, and then I'll write them on the signs."

"Thanks." Ana grabbed the list, scratched off her name and put Ash's on it instead, not feeling one bit of guilt about it. Mavis paid no attention to her as she finished the signs. "Can I help you?"

"Yes. Take these over to the large barrels that were placed along the wall where the food tables are, and stick them on with these tacks. Then hope for dimes and dollars from heaven!"

"Hey, beautiful," she heard as she put the first sign up. She glanced up at Tighe.

"Hi. Why aren't you off being the prize?"

"There's three more bachelors to auction. My winner went off with friends, and I needed a chance to breathe. It's hard being hunk of the night."

"I'm sure. Help me put all these signs up." She

handed Tighe half the signs and finished what she'd been doing. "Were you surprised by how much you went for?"

"Nah," Tighe said. "I pretty much had to go for double to make up for what Dante won't bring in."

She laughed. "That's mean."

"It's true, though. He won't give the ladies what they want." He shook his head. "Dante likes to hide his inner wolf, and I like to set mine free."

"You certainly gave the ladies a lot to consider." She smiled at the signs she'd put up. "How'd you see through my disguise?"

"Didn't. Ash told me to come keep an eye on you."

Ana looked at him. "Why?"

"Didn't ask. Just did what I was told, as I always do." He grinned. "She also told me that my twin gave you some money to bid on him with."

People milled past, looking at the names on the barrels, tossing in money for their favorite finalist.

"This is a great idea," a woman said to Ana. "I hope Diablo will put on another masquerade ball for next year! It's fun to have a Christmas ball. It's like a Victorian Christmas come to life."

Ana smiled, and the lady and her gentleman moved on. "That'll make Fiona happy."

"Fiona was happy when I went for a princely sum. All she can see is that new roof. Next year it'll be new computers for the classrooms or something." He smiled at her, all wolf. "Give me my brother's money."

"Why?"

"Because you won't need it. He'll probably go for about fifty bucks."

Ana laughed. "You're terrible." She took the money from her gold purse that matched the high heel gold pumps that had appeared in her closet along with the splendid dress, and handed it to Tighe.

"Ah, my twin. Always overestimating himself," he said, looking sorrowfully at the money. He tossed all of it into the barrel labeled Tighe.

Ana gasped. "Tighe!"

He laughed. "Look at it this way. Maybe I'll be high score twice tonight."

"But what will I tell Dante when he asks where his money went?"

Tighe smiled, pure wolf. "That I said, 'May the best man win.'"

She couldn't help laughing. "He's going to be mad at you."

"Nope. Not me. No one can ever stay mad at me for long. Hey, I'm going to get some punch—want one?"

"Yes, thanks."

"With rum, or without?"

She shook her head, not entirely shocked by Tighe's offer. "You know you're not allowed to do that. Fiona says this is a no-alcohol night for us."

"We can't be role models all the time. Anyway, punch and rum go together like kisses and soft skin," Tighe said, heading to the punch table.

"Excuse me," she heard.

Ana turned to face Sawyer Cash, who made no effort to conceal her identity. Her domino hung from her arm.

"Yes?" Ana said.

"Where did Tighe run off to? I'd like to talk to him."

"He should be back in a moment."

"Thank you. Are you bidding tonight?"

Ana shook her head. "No."

"Fortunately, there's another Callahan up for grabs.

I've got my heart set on winning another one. A lady's fantasy to spend an evening with twin hunks, right?"

Dante. Ana checked over the barrels one last time, satisfied that the signs were properly attached. "I need to head back to help with the committee. Good night."

Ana hurried off before she said something she'd regret. Sawyer hadn't known who she was or she probably wouldn't have spoken so freely. Ana decided not to let it bother her—she had to find Dante and let him know that his money had gone into Tighe's barrel.

The next auction was starting up, and Fiona was clearly in her element. Ana didn't recognize the cowboy bachelor on the stage, but he was doing his best to compete with the bar Tighe had set, and the ladies seemed to appreciate his efforts.

"Hello, lady in red," Galen said. "Having fun?"

"The evening certainly seems to be a success."

He grinned. "The aunt is raking it in. Ashlyn wants me to stick to you like glue."

"Why?"

"Jace thought he saw some of Wolf's minions." Galen shrugged. "Maybe he did, maybe he didn't, but Ash is protective."

"I'm a bodyguard, I can handle myself. Please don't worry about me."

He held up a hand. "No one's worrying. But Callahans take care of their own." He gave her an easy smile. "I hear there may be a little Callahan on the way. Ash would maim me if I didn't guard him with my life."

"You can't tell Dante!" She was annoyed with Ash for spilling her secret. "I'm going to kill Ashlyn!"

"She wouldn't have said anything except that Jace got her nervous. Your secret is safe with me." He smiled at her kindly. "If Fiona had half a clue you're expecting, Dante wouldn't be on the block tonight, that's for sure."

"I wouldn't want to change a thing," Ana said quickly. "I hope he brings in a ton of money."

"Nah," Galen said, "Tighe's the rainmaker. Dante's more likely to get rained out. He just doesn't have the wild side in him anymore. He used to. I wondered what had settled him down, thought maybe he'd rattled his brains too much when he was chasing buckles. I never suspected it might have been you who was responsible for taming my brother."

"I don't want to tame him," Ana said with spirit. "Dante is fine just the way he is."

"I think you should tell him before he makes an ass of himself on the stage," Galen said. "No new father should be shaking his stuff for other women."

Ana shook her head, laughing. "I'm really not worried, Galen. Thanks. I'll tell him after Christmas."

"Why then?"

"Because we're both going in separate directions. It will be safe."

"I don't like it," Galen said, and Dante said, "Don't like what? Is this blockhead bothering you, miss?"

Ana hesitated. Galen slapped Dante on the back and laughed.

"I cede the lady to you, Dante. Try not to make her run for the exit." Galen went off, still chuckling to himself.

Dante looked at Ana. "Hi."

"Hi," Ana said.

"You're gorgeous." He gazed at her, taking in every inch of the gown. "Ash told me that you found a dress, and you certainly did. You're the most beautiful woman here, Ana."

"Thank you." She smiled at Dante. "You don't look so bad yourself. Are you ready to be the grand prize?"

He grimaced. "I'm going to tell Aunt Fiona I have stage fright."

"You can't." Ana couldn't help laughing.

"Anyway, I'm the winner no matter what," Dante said. "I had the smarts to make certain the most beautiful woman in the room takes me home tonight."

"About that—" Ana began, but Jace came by, slapping his brother on the back.

"Don't chat up gorgeous blondes," Jace told Dante. "Leave that for me. Hello, beautiful. Don't waste your time on this guy—"

"Jace," Dante interrupted, "this is Ana."

"Oh." Jace looked startled. "Really?"

She nodded. "Hi, Jace."

"Wow." He gave her a long, considering look. "Jeez, Dante, I should have known you'd hog the best woman around." He sighed dramatically. "Oh, well, easy come, easy go. Off I go."

Dante shook his head. "Always a drama king."

"Corinne is waving at me. She must need help." Ana looked at Dante one last time. "Good luck, Dante."

"I don't need luck," he said. "I need you—"

Ash dragged Ana off. "Whew, my brothers are windy. Come on, Corinne wants us to hand out some grab bags."

"Grab bags?"

"Goody bags. Advertising, candy, gift cards, a couple bags have some prizes in them. Fiona never misses a chance to advertise the wonder that is Diablo."

Ana followed. "Ash, I have a bone to pick with you. You told Galen!"

"Yeah, but only so he'd keep an eye on you. Galen

won't say anything. He looks like he's not very deep but he is."

"Actually, I think Galen looks very deep, and you still weren't supposed to tell! Now two people in Dante's family know before he does, and it isn't right."

"That may be. Dante's sensitive, gets his feelings hurt easily. You probably should tell him as soon as possible." She handed Ana a tray of goody bags. "Just pass those out, one per person."

"Ash—"

"Don't be shy. Every woman will want one, and sometimes the guys do, too. There's plenty to go around." Ash gave her a tiny push toward the library. "Off you go. And stay away from Wolf. We hear he might be around somewhere. Don't worry, Galen's keeping an eye on things, but just the same, if you see Wolf, tell him to buzz off."

Ana decided she'd chastise Ash about spilling her secret later, though she doubted it would do much good. "Buzz off," she murmured, "that'll be effective." She went off with her tray of green and red wrapped bags, delighted when they were eagerly snapped up by anyone who saw them.

"Excuse me," Sawyer said, taking two off her tray. "When does the bidding start for the grand prize?"

"Midnight. Hope you brought a full pocketbook," Ana said, tempted to tell Sawyer about the fact that Dante was going to be a father, but opting not to wreck Fiona's secret fundraising weapon.

"I heard he's going to strip down to his whatevers," Sawyer said, and Ana laughed.

"I very much doubt it. Good luck with that." She went on with her tray, feeling slightly guilty that she hadn't told Dante that his money was gone.

"Hey," Dante said, stopping her as she went to go get more bags, "stop and talk to me for a second."

"I can't talk too long, and besides which, the rumor's going around that you're doing a striptease tonight."

He snorted. "Not hardly."

She smiled. "The ladies are holding back on their bidding waiting for the grand prize. You're going to have to do something to earn your coin."

"Listen." He glanced around at the eager crowd. "Can we talk?"

"Now?"

"If Fiona can spare you." He glanced around and then hustled her into a corner past the stage stairs. "Ana, this auction thing doesn't mean anything to me. I hope you know that."

She was surprised. "It means a lot to your aunt, Dante."

"No, I know that." He looked at her. "Take off your mask so I can see your face."

She didn't move, so he did it for her, and he smiled. "Let's run off together."

Her heart skipped. "Run off?"

"Dodge this shindig. Fiona's raking in cash, she doesn't need me."

"No way. You stay and be an excellent finale."

His gaze found her lips, traveled back up to her eyes. "I'm going to pawn it off on Jace. He'll make a good grand prize. And it will serve him right."

Ana shook her head. "My advice is that you make the most of it. You're just trying to talk me into getting you out of it because you're nervous you won't fetch as much as Tighe did."

He looked outraged. "There's no way my twin has more appeal than me."

She laughed. "One thing you Callahans do not lack for is ego."

"So I can't talk you into running off with me?"

"No, because you're just trying to get out of your job, which I don't admire in the least. By the way, about your money—"

"That reminds me. I'm going to give you a couple hundred more bucks, just in case." Reaching into his wallet, he dragged out eight hundred-dollar bills. "If the bidding goes higher, you'll have to cover me."

"What?" Ana laughed out loud. "I'm not about to float you a two-thousand-dollar loan, Callahan."

"I expect you to be creative."

He was so handsome she thought there was a lot she could be creative about with him. "Like how?"

"Put out a rumor about me." He glanced around, made sure no one could hear. "Say something that'll bring down the bidding."

She blinked. "I thought you said you'd go for more than Tighe any day of the week."

"I would. But I don't have to."

"Wouldn't you hate to be a dud grand prize? Isn't your Callahan ego on the line?"

He shrugged. "I'll just make up the difference to Aunt Fiona out of my own pocket for the elementary school roof."

Ana narrowed her gaze, considered him. "You want me to help you throw your bidding?"

"I don't have any more cash on me," Dante said. "I'd give you four grand to win me, but I don't carry that kind of dough in my back pocket. All I had was the thousand I gave you."

"Not even that much," Ana said. "Tighe tossed the money you gave me into his barrel."

"What?"

"Yes," Ana said, "maybe you could find an ATM? Write a check?"

Dante's face was a study in outrage. "I'm going to kill my weasel twin."

"You can't," Ana said, "you have to congratulate him for outwitting you. That's what a Callahan does."

"Not this one," Dante said. "I rode Firefreak for my twin when he was having his existential meltdown. I've had his back in remote corners of the world, I—"

"Blah, blah, blah," Ana said. "If you want to beat him, you'll have to figure it out. I suggest you jump on stage and dance like you're on a hot stove."

He shook his head at her. "You're not helping at all. A woman isn't supposed to encourage a man to—"

"Win? Aren't you two supposed to be the competitors in the family? So beat him."

He touched her cheek with one finger. "You're not going to help me, are you?"

"I am helping. I'm encouraging you to do your very best," Ana said. "Believe me, I could sandbag you and take you home. I could spread a rumor about you that would ensure you wouldn't get a single bid. But I prefer to see you bring in the most money possible for Fiona's charity."

He looked intrigued. "What kind of rumor would you spread that would keep me from getting a bid?"

She wasn't going to tell everything. "For starters, that you're a terrible kisser."

"I am not!"

She laughed. "Says who?"

"Look, lady. If you want me to win, if you want me to be a grand prize with oomph, give my ego something to crow about. Don't crush it."

"Well," Ana said, "I could say you're a werewolf, and that on full moons you climb trees. People would believe anything of the Callahans."

"True," he conceded, "but I still think I'd get bids. A woman would think she could tame my inner wolf."

"All right. I could spread the rumor that you're going to be a father. That would dampen the ladies' enthusiasm, don't you think?"

He laughed. "Of the three, I'd go with the werewolf story. It's the only one anybody might possibly believe." He kissed her on the forehead. "Thanks for the encouragement. I'm ready now to do my duty."

"That's nice," Ana said, slightly miffed that Dante hadn't even given an iota of credence to the idea that he might be a father. "Good luck."

"I expect praise when I bring home the bacon," Dante said. "In fact, plan on taking me out to dinner to celebrate."

He went off, his ego fully restored, apparently. Ana sighed, put her mask back on and stared at the eight hundred dollars he'd given her.

It wouldn't be enough. She knew that. Not a woman had moved from the theater as they waited for midnight, the hour the "Grand Prize" went on stage.

Ten minutes.

Ten minutes until another woman won Dante.

She tossed the money into Tighe's barrel.

Chapter Fifteen

Ash went by, carrying a tray, and Ana grabbed her arm. "If I was to bid at the auction, can I pay with a check, Ash?"

Ashlyn raised a brow. "You're not going to bid on my brother, are you?"

Ana shrugged. "I'm considering it."

"What are you thinking of doing?"

"Nothing." Ana didn't want to share her thoughts.

"If you tell me, I'll help," Ash said.

"I don't know if I can trust you. You told Galen about the baby, and I'm afraid he's going to tell Dante before I do!"

Ash grinned, looking elfin and mischievous with her silver-blond hair curling around her face and her mask on. "You *are* going to bid on him!"

"If I can write a check, I might."

"Fiona would take a check from you," Ash said, "she knows you."

"Okay." Ana took a deep breath, thought through her best scenarios. She didn't want to use Dante's money to bid; if she was going to do this, she wanted to do it on her own, with her own funds. "What did the grand prize go for last year?"

"I'm not sure we had one. Frankly, I think Fiona's just trying to smoke you out."

Ana's eyes widened. "You mean this is a setup?"

"Well, I wouldn't put it past Fiona to try to flush you out into the open." Ash smiled. "I mean think of it. You'd see all these women throwing themselves at my handsome brother, you'd get jealous, start rethinking your notion of not wanting to be tied down—"

"I never said I didn't want to be tied down. Dante is the commitmentphobe. Although my parents aren't married. They were, but now they're not. They live in separate houses, and they get along better than ever. We have holidays together and everything. Sometimes marriage isn't all it's cracked up to be. I'm okay with it." She took a deep breath. "Dante never said he loved me, or that he cared about me. I wanted a child more than anything in the world, and I knew Dante was my kind of father material. If I held out for marriage, I'd be holding my breath forever."

"Wow," Ash said, her eyes huge behind the mask, "how come you never told me any of that before?"

"Because you're a blabbermouth," Ana said, teasing. "You don't keep any secrets from your brothers."

"I do, too." Ash glanced around at the excited women pushing toward the stage, waiting for Dante to come out. "I'm just not very good at it, is all."

"Like when you go to the canyons when you're not supposed to."

"That wasn't my fault. My brothers would have never found out about that, if Xav and I hadn't gotten tied up. I still think it was some of Uncle Wolf's goons," she said on a whisper, "but I'm starting to get suspicious of that Sawyer girl, too."

"I thought you said it was men who tied you guys up."

"Yeah. But I heard a woman's voice, too. Could have been her. I don't like the way she's bidding on my brothers." Ashlyn frowned. "I think that's a setup, too."

"What, Sawyer's going to win one of the guys and get cozy with him and sweet-talk him out of all the family secrets? Like Mata Hari or something?"

"You laugh," Ashlyn said, "but what other reason would she have for suddenly showing up and throwing herself at my adorably hot brothers?" Ash shook her head. "I don't like it."

"Anyway," Ana said, not wanting to delve further into Ash's theories, "I haven't decided to bid. I just wanted to know how it works."

"Yeah, well, I think all you have to do is raise your paddle, girlfriend. No big deal. Although then you have to decide what you'd do with him if you do win him." Ash winked at her. "I'll try to help you out if I see you waving your paddle around."

"Uh, thanks." Ana wasn't sure she needed any help from Ash. It wasn't always a good thing, since Ash was as tricky as her aunt Fiona. Ash went off with her tray, and Ana went into a side room to pull her phone from her purse to check her account, see what she could afford to pony up for a hot cowboy—and the father of her child.

There was terrible reception in this tiny room. She managed to pull up her account—five thousand dollars was all she had to her name. Ana closed her eyes for a second.

It would be worth every penny if she spent it to win Dante. He'd wanted her to rescue him. Maybe it was the best thing to do.

Who was she kidding? It would be a dream fantasy to win him any way she could get him.

"All right," Ana said, "I'll do it."

She slid her phone into her small gold bag, hesitating when she heard a click behind her. Whirling, she saw that she was still alone in the room. Hurrying to the door, she tried to open it.

Locked.

She banged on the door. "Hey! I'm in here!"

Of course no one came. "Because that would be too easy since I just made up my mind to go get the man of my dreams," she muttered, pulling out her cell phone.

It wasn't quite dead—close, but not completely dead—but there wasn't any reception now. No windows, and the door locked, a room not much bigger than a laundry room. Ana banged on the door again, knowing that the room was too far down the hall from the noisy stage. Her banging couldn't be heard, at least not over the music and excited chatter of so many people. It was a party after all, and Fiona wouldn't have wanted her party to be a quiet affair.

Ana took off her mask. She didn't like being shut up in small, airless rooms, and she was cranky at being bested by someone. When she found out who'd locked her in here right before the grand prize auction, they were going to have some serious explaining to do.

DANTE GLANCED AT ASH before he went up on the stage, his heart jumping. "I don't see Ana."

"She's around somewhere. Go," Ash told him. "Be amazing. Get the dough, brother. You can do it." She straightened his tux tie, and he grimaced impatiently.

"Ana should be here. Go find her, Ash. Please."

"And leave you? No way. Every guy needs his sister.

Besides, I have it from Ana's own mouth that she'll be here to watch you smash all previous records."

He didn't want to get on stage. He didn't want to be auctioned. Why had he let his aunt and brother goad him into this? "I'm about to forfeit and just donate a few grand to Fiona's roof project. I could claim that I just became engaged and am therefore ineligible to take another lady out."

"You could," Ash said, "but that would be a lie."

It would be a lie, but not a huge one. He'd love to be engaged to Ana, if he could ever settle the woman down. She was harder to slow down than…than he was.

"Maybe that's why I like her so much," he muttered, and Ash said, "What?"

"Nothing. Please go find Ana."

She shook her head. "Pitiful."

"Yeah, but I really don't have a problem with that."

Ash sighed in disgust. "If you like Ana so much, why don't you tell her?"

How did one explain such things to their little sister? "Look, for the first year and a half that Ana was here, she barely gave me the time of day. I would have sworn up and down that she didn't want anything to do with me, while all the way she and River acted like Jace was the cat's meow."

"They treat him like a kid brother."

"True, but—" He glanced around. "Please go find my girl."

"Your girl?"

"Yes. She's got a lot of my money, and I want to see it spent."

"Pathetic," Ash said. "I'm not going to hunt Ana up. If she wanted to be here, she would. If she was smart, she'd take your money and go vacation in Canada."

"At this time of year? Too dang cold when she could be right here with me warming her up." He glanced around, realizing that Fiona was waving at him to get on stage. "Please find her. Mavis or Corinne have probably got her stuck in a kissing booth or something. Anything for a buck around here. But I don't want to be won by anyone but Ana," he told his sister. "Just like you wouldn't want to be won by anyone but Xav."

"That's not fair," Ash murmured. "Anyway, I'm not dumb enough to put myself in a position to be with anyone but him. Even if he doesn't really want to be in said position with me, I'm pretty sure I'm wearing him down."

Dante patted his sister's shoulder. "You could wear down a saint, sister. Go find my bodyguard and tell her it's time for her to protect someone. Namely me."

He got on the stage, scooted behind the curtain where Fiona pointed for him to stand so he could make a grand entrance.

"Be electrifying," Fiona told him. "I'm looking for you to bring in a big haul."

"Aunt Fiona," Dante said, "let me just give you whatever Tighe went for and call it even, okay?"

His aunt's eyes were huge. She opened the curtain a crack. "Do you see all those man-starved women out there? They've hung around until the stroke of midnight to win you. You can't let them down! They want their handsome prince!"

Of course he was no prince, was he? If he was, he'd catch a bodyguard princess. Ana sure had looked like one tonight, but then again, he'd had a thing for her since she'd first come to Rancho Diablo. A quick scan of the front rows of excited women revealed that there was no red-gowned female with a mysterious black mask waiting to rescue him, even though he'd given her the means to do so.

He sighed, nodded at his aunt. "Lead me to the slaughter."

"Such an attitude!" Fiona shook her head. "Any right-thinking, red-blooded male would give his best saddle to have so many women vying for his attention."

"True," Dante said, "but nobody has ever accused me of right-thinking."

"You'll get in the swing of it when the bright light hits you," Fiona said. "Goodness knows I thought Tighe was going to die of stage fright."

"Really?"

Aunt Fiona rolled her eyes. "No, but I'm trying to give you a little mental energy, nephew. You're flat as a pancake. Makes it hard for me to sell you when I get out there. And we're only short the full cost of the roof by about five grand!" She looked at him. "Picture the number five in your mind's eye, followed by three zeroes. Now go get it!"

She shoved him onto the stage, the spotlight hit him, women shrieked and squealed, the music roared to a fever pitch—and something happened to Dante, pretty much like when Firefreak had cannoned forward out of the chute—he went into survival mode.

ASH GLANCED AROUND WILDLY for Ana, not seeing her in the crowd. "Jace, go find Ana. She's probably still parceling out goody bags. She's going to miss the auction!"

"Does she care?" Jace demanded.

Ash gave him a sisterly punch in the side. "Of course she cares! What woman doesn't care about the father of her child getting auctioned off to another woman?"

"What father of what child?" Jace asked, sounding stunned, and Ash clapped her hand over her mouth.

"Never mind," Ash said.

Jace's eyes were huge. Around them, women jostled and shoved to get closer to the stage, where Dante was gyrating and dancing to make a puppet blush. The ladies were eating it up, and paddles were flashing furiously as Fiona egged on the bids. "Go find her! Hurry!"

"Is Ana pregnant with Dante's baby?" Jace asked.

"Yes, and if you don't go find her, you're never going to be able to get a lady pregnant, if you get my drift!" Ash glared at him. "Go!"

"Hell's bell's, Ash!" Jace said, streaking off.

Sawyer Cash was clearly not to be outdone. She and the rose gown that had annoyed Ana were in a bidding war, the bids going over two thousand. Dante tossed his hat into the crowd, then a handful of kisses. Ash rolled her eyes, wondered how to stop the train that was bearing down on her dunce of a brother. "Really, all of them are dunces," she muttered. "It's such a shame."

Maybe those two would run out of cash soon. Perhaps there was a dark horse who hadn't yet bid. Ana wouldn't be happy about either of these women going out on a date with Dante. She glanced at the door, hoping to see Jace returning with Ana.

Maybe Ana wouldn't bid, though. She was stubborn that way. Ash had never seen two people who were so right for each other fight it so hard. But there was a baby to consider.

Of course Dante didn't know about that. If he did, he'd be hell-bent for leather to get Ana to the altar.

Which was exactly what Ana didn't want. Ash understood that—she wouldn't want a man to want to marry her just because she was pregnant, either. No woman wanted that!

The bidding went over three thousand dollars, Fiona practically crowing her excitement over the microphone. Dante undid his tie, tossed it aside, undid three buttons on his shirt, then in what Ash thought was a remarkable return to his wild side, Dante ripped his shirt off with a flourish.

The room erupted, at least ten more paddles furiously waving with bids, encouraging her brother to make an even bigger donkey of himself. Something had to be done. Dante didn't need to be on a date with anyone but Ana, in Ash's estimation.

But what to do? Grab Fiona's microphone and make an announcement that Dante was expecting a child he didn't know about? That would sure silence the bidding. The women would evaporate like water on a stove.

But that wouldn't be fair to Ana. She'd promised not to tell Dante. Or anyone for that matter, though she'd had a slip here and there. Still, she couldn't do it.

There had to be another way.

She eyed the fire alarm on the far wall of the packed theater. It was against the law, of course. Punishable by fines and probably some time in Sheriff Cartwright's jail.

Sometimes, you had to stand for something—it was live by the sword, die by the sword.

On stage Dante flexed his muscles like a bodybuilder, and the women went crazy. Something had to be done to save her brother from himself.

Ash took a deep breath.

ANA PERKED UP WHEN SHE thought she heard someone calling her name. "In here!" She banged fiercely on the door. "I'm in here!"

Jace opened the door. "Ana! Why are you in the old theater prop room?"

"Is that what this is?"

"It was before everything was rebuilt. Now I think it's a storage closet." He frowned. "You're missing Dante, and Ash says you better hurry." He looked at her. "Is it true that you're pregnant with Dante's baby?"

"I— Oh, Jace, don't tell anyone, all right? I need to talk to Dante first." She went running down the hall into the theater. "Five thousand dollars!" Ana yelled at the top of her lungs. "I bid five... What happened? Why is everyone standing around? Is the auction over?"

The entire roomful of women turned to gawk at her. On stage, Dante stared at her. The music had stopped and the room was silent as an empty cave, her loud announcement as she'd dashed into the room echoing to all four corners.

Dante took the microphone from his aunt. "Ana, is there something you want to tell me?"

Ana glanced at Ashlyn, shocked.

"I'm sorry, Ana! I had to do something!" Ash's face wasn't exactly apologetic, but she did look very worried. "It was tell the truth or pull the fire alarm, and I really didn't want to go to jail at Christmas!"

The ladies burst into dismayed chatter as Dante left the stage. Seeing her big jackpot slip away, Fiona called, "Don't leave unhappy, ladies! Luckily I have—" She quickly glanced around, her gaze falling on her nephews. "Galen, come on up! Jace, you, too! We've got women here who want a date with a handsome *unattached* Callahan cowboy, and fortunately, I can offer you two for the price of one! How's that for an even better grand prize?"

Galen glanced at Jace, who'd stuck close to Ana as she'd dashed down the hall. "I spent enough time serving my country and going to med school that I can't think of anything more wonderful than going out with a beautiful woman who wants to buy me. What do you think, Jace?" Galen asked.

Jace grinned. "I'm game. Look at all those hot ladies." Then he yelled, "I say let the bidding begin!"

He hopped on stage and Galen followed with enthusiasm, and the room erupted in cheers. Fiona looked like she said, "Phew," but Ana felt no relief at all as Dante bore down on her, his handsome face not happy at all. He finished buttoning his shirt up as he approached. "When were you going to tell me?"

"After Christmas," Ana said.

"As we both went our separate ways?"

She put up her chin. "Seemed like the right thing to do."

"The right thing to do," Dante said, "is get married. Tonight."

Chapter Sixteen

Poleaxed wasn't quite a good enough word to describe how Dante felt when Ash shouted out that he was expecting a baby. Fiona had nearly dropped her microphone, the entire room had gone up in a whoosh of "Oh, no!" and he'd nearly…well, he'd stood tacked to the floor. Poleaxed and dumbfounded.

Joy swept him.

Then annoyance. Ana hadn't told him.

But then she'd rushed into the room, shouting that she was bidding five grand for him, and he'd felt a lot better.

He still wasn't happy with her.

Ana glared at him, clearly not pleased with his proposal. "By the way, thanks for the bid. Appreciate knowing that you think so highly of me. Come on, beautiful, let's get out of here. People are gossiping, and we really want their attention on Jace and Galen. Fiona's got some making up to do, now that her grand prize defaulted."

"Getting out of here is fine," Ana said, "after I figure out who locked me into that room." She frowned, displeased and cute, he thought. "Someone didn't want me to win you."

He grinned. "Can you blame them?"

She was in no mood to be teased as she swept out of the theater into the street. "Dante, I don't want to hear another word about marriage. Let's just get that straight right now."

"You're sweet, not wanting to tie me down and all, but don't worry." He smiled at Ana, his most winning smile. "This prince fully intends to ride to your rescue."

"You don't seem to understand," Ana said. "I just rescued you."

"And I appreciate it."

"You didn't look like you were suffering too much." He followed her over to the barrels, where she checked the money "votes" in each of them. "If I hadn't known better, I would have thought you were interviewing to become a stripper."

"Oh," he said, drawing her into his arms, "you're jealous. No need to be, though. You've won me fair and square." He looked down at her. "Are we really having a baby?"

"Yes," Ana said, looking slightly irritated, "we are. I'm planning to name him Jonathan Dante, unless you have a different idea." She wouldn't look at him, and he thought that didn't bode well for him.

"I don't really care. I'm having a son." He laughed out loud. "I'm having a son!"

"Yes, we are. Well, it might be a girl. But anyway, I wouldn't have told you like this, but clearly Ash can't keep a secret. Not that I can blame it on her." She sighed. "I should have told you sooner."

Ash came speeding around the corner, out of breath as she reached Ana. "I am so sorry! It was either disqualify my brother or pull the fire alarm, and I didn't want to go to jail, so—" She looked at her brother. "You may have been on the way to a new record, brother. I was impressed, in spite of myself. I had no idea you could dance like that."

"Yes," Ana said, "I didn't know, either."

Oh, his angel cake was just a bit miffed that he'd been strutting for the ladies. "I knew you'd arrive any second to rescue me."

"You didn't," Ash said, "you didn't give her near enough money. Face it, you were going home with someone else."

"And all your money is in Tighe's barrel," Ana said. "He said he wanted to win this part of the evening, too."

He touched Ana's cheek. "He didn't win anything. I'm having a baby." Then he laughed. "This is awesome. I can't believe it."

"Congratulations." His sister thumped him on his back. "Really didn't know there was so much wild man left in you anymore."

"Yeah, well." He wasn't sure what to say to his sister's ribbing. Ana didn't look impressed, so he hoped she'd drop that thought and move on.

"Ash," Ana said, "someone locked me in the theater prop room so I couldn't bid on Dante."

Ash's eyes went round. "Are you sure?"

"The door was locked."

Dante shook his head. "Let's not focus on that right now. Let's focus on getting married."

"Dante, I'm not marrying you," Ana said, her voice sure.

"Well, here's where I disappear," Ash said. "Glad you got out of the prop closet in time to… Oh, never mind," she said, when Ana and Dante glared at her.

"I'll go see if Jace and Galen are holding up the family rep."

His sister drifted off. "Come on, beautiful. Let's dance, at least, okay?" He drew her into his arms. "You know, Cinderella left the ball at midnight, and left her shoe as a calling card. The prince had to search high and low for her." The music from the theater and the ongoing auction spilled onto the street, which was lit with lovely white lights. Christmas wreaths hung in every shop window. "I'm not going to let you get away from me, even if you are being a stubborn thing."

Ana gasped. "Your auction was at midnight!"

"Yeah. It's twelve-thirty now. Why?"

She glanced down at her dress as if to make sure it was still on her. "I—just wondered."

He blinked. "Wait a minute! You're wearing the magic wedding dress!"

She nodded. "Yes, I am."

His gaze swept her. "That dress *disappeared*."

"It was in my closet. Somehow."

"But it disappeared. Poofed right out of my hands."

She looked confused. "Your hands? What do you have to do with my gown?"

"Fiona sent me upstairs to put it in the closet. This was after we saw you sprinting across the yard. You were crying, weren't you?" It felt so good to hold Ana in his arms. He'd waited a long time to hold her close, dance with her, talk to her. Now she was going to have his baby. How lucky could a guy get? "What made you cry that day, babe?"

"Fiona told me I'd see the man of my dreams, that one man who was right for me," Ana said, her voice soft. "But I didn't see anyone. And then this gown turned red!" She looked up at him. "It's beautiful, fairy-tale, perfect for tonight, but it's not my idea of a dream wedding gown. And I was kind of hoping I'd see my handsome prince."

"I don't know what to say to that."

"It's a Callahan tradition, you know. You should have more idea about it than I do."

He danced her into a more private enclave where not as many people milled about. "The good news is that the way the legend works is that when a baby is in the picture, it doesn't matter if you saw your prince or not. You've already got him."

"That's sweet," she murmured, "but I don't know if it's true. I think you're just saying that. You were all ready to ride off into the sunset and hit the rodeo circuit again."

"Yeah, because I didn't know you were crazy for me." His heart felt as if it was going to beat out of his chest. "You are, aren't you?"

"Dante, I don't know if we're meant to be. That's the hardest part of this. A baby doesn't make it love."

This was true. He got that she was worried that he was just saying things to convince her to marry him. Wasn't that what all the Callahans did? Ran real hard to catch their lady—when they finally realized they wanted to be caught themselves?

"Maybe we give it some time. Like maybe until tomorrow," Dante said, and Ana laughed, and he felt better. It would all work out. They were meant to be together, and it didn't matter about legends or magic or anything. They were right enough together to make a baby. "I can't believe I'm going to be a father."

"You're not even going to ask me about the fact that we always used a condom, are you?"

He shook his head. "I'm quite capable of keeping

you as pregnant as you want to be. I look forward to the challenge. Nothing better than a grail for a man to pit himself against."

"There is never a time when Callahan ego is at low ebb, is there?"

"Not often." What did a man have beside his pride, the psyche inside him that strove for courage? He wanted to hold her closer than he could at the moment, but he thought he was feeling a bit of resistance from her, too. That was all right. He knew how to be patient. Oh, patience was hard, when he was as crazy about Ana as he was. In the end, believing she would come to him because she trusted he was the man for her would make everything that much more perfect. "I'd invite you back to my place, but you'll have to marry me first. Make an honest man of me."

She gasped. "Did you just do something to my zipper?"

He shook his head. "No, gorgeous. But I will be happy to do something to your zipper if you want me to—"

Her eyes were huge. "Dante, I need to go."

"Okay, I'll—"

"No, you have to stay here by the barrels. When your brothers' auctions are done—any minute now—the guys and ladies who are finalists will come out to see who won. You're going to have to judge which of these barrels are most full for the guy, and one for the girl."

"I'm sure not picking Tighe," he said, "even if he did get all my money."

Ana looked desperate. He couldn't figure out what was going on with her. "Is something wrong, Ana?"

"I'm not sure." She glanced down at her dress, then gasped. "Dante, I have to go!"

"Where?"

"Home," she said, and then she took off running.

"Holy smokes," Dante muttered. "Talk about giving a guy a complex."

Tighe walked by, then punched him in the arm. "Talking to yourself?"

"A little. Not as much as I might be in a moment." He glanced around, realizing the partygoers were spilling forth from the theater.

"Did you run Ana off?"

"I don't think so."

"You don't know?" his twin asked. "Either she was giving you good vibrations, or you were getting bad atmospherics from her. Which was it?"

"I'm not sure," Dante said, not happy.

Tighe shook his head. "Dude, is that a shoe?"

He looked where his twin was pointing. In the road, in the middle of the square was, indeed, a golden pump. Ana's. "That's odd. No woman runs off without her shoe. Ladies prize their shoes as if they are actually gold."

"She must have *really* wanted to get away from you," Tighe observed. "It's funny, isn't it? Women run to me, they run away from you."

Dante picked up the shoe, not sure what to make of the mother of his child being so anxious to get away from him that she took off barefoot, especially in the snow. "When I marry her, I'm going to make her wear cowboy boots with her wedding dress. She can't slip out of cowboy boots that easily, not without making a heckuva scene." He laughed, and Tighe sighed dolefully.

"You are so weird you deserve everything you get," Tighe said. "I'll man the barrel contest and pick the winners. You go after Ana before her case of second thoughts gets set in stone."

"You want to oversee this to make sure you win," Dante said, and Tighe said, "Yeah, but do you really care?"

He really didn't. "Knock yourself out. Pick a female winner, and a male winner, and good luck. With Sawyer, that is."

"What's that supposed to mean?"

"I don't know," Dante said. "Just feels like bad juju to be mixed up with anybody related to Storm. But good luck with that." He loped off after Ana. Maybe if he hurried, he could catch her in time to talk her into staying in the hot gown and heading to Vegas with him for an early morning, presto-change-o hitching.

Nothing would make him happier.

IN A PANIC, ANA RAN into her room at Rancho Diablo, trying desperately to shrug out of the magic wedding dress. Something was happening to it. She could feel the fabric shifting, as though it might disappear any moment, leaving her naked. She'd felt the seams sort of quivering, and the zipper somehow warming, as if it wanted to melt away at the masquerade ball. When she'd looked down and realized the hem was evanescing and the golden pumps vanishing, she'd known she had to get home before the magic completely deserted her.

Gasping, she barely made it into her bedroom and slammed the door before the gown filtered away completely. Gone.

She grabbed a robe and kicked off the one pump,

which was no longer gold and beautiful. "Oh, no," she murmured, sadly eying the remnant of the splendid shoe. "You were only a mirage, after all."

She pulled off her mask, laying it on her dresser. The enchanted evening was over. Dante knew he was going to be a father. When had she realized how much she loved him?

When they'd been kidnapped and forced to walk to get away from their captors. He'd been so kind and considerate.

Of course, he also loved to tease her. His raffish side was one of the things she liked most about him.

She'd never dreamed she could become pregnant. And with him, it had been so easy.

Almost magical.

But she wanted to be with him forever. She wanted to marry Dante, be his wife, love him, take care of him, raise their baby together. It was such a beautiful dream that it put tears in her eyes.

A knock on her door sent her grabbing for jeans and a shirt. "Who is it?"

"Dante. Can I talk to you for a minute?"

She opened the door. "Hi."

"Hi." He smiled, and her heart jumped wildly. "You forgot this," he said, handing her the golden pump that had fallen off as she'd run to escape finding herself nude in the town square.

"Thanks." She took it from him.

"You left really fast."

"I know." She didn't know what to make of the fact that the dress had disappeared—what was the meaning behind that? So she didn't say anything else.

"You know, in the fairy tale, when the prince found

Cinderella and brought the magic slipper to her, they lived happily ever after."

She looked at him. "It's not quite the same. You didn't have to search for me."

He shrugged. "Feels like I'm always searching for you."

"I'm right here. I've been at Rancho Diablo for over a year, nearly two."

He tipped his hat back. "Yeah, but strangely, it seems that whenever I get remotely close to you, you disappear. Or the dress disappears. We get kidnapped."

"None of that is generated by me. Except for when I went home, but I hadn't been home in a while, so you can't really hold that against me."

"All right." He picked up her hand, brushed it across his lips, sending a tingle all over her. "Let's prove that nothing else is going to come between us."

She took a deep breath. "You're going to say we should head to Vegas and get married."

"Yeah. Then it's just you, and me, and baby. Nothing comes between us. We work out all the difficulties after we say I do."

"Dante," Ana said, "why did you go on the rodeo circuit?"

He sat on the bed, pulled her into his lap. "To save my brother from himself."

"You went," Ana said, "because you're the kind of man who doesn't like to settle in one place."

"Actually, I went to keep my mind off of you, gorgeous."

"That's not true," Ana protested. "You'd barely talked to me before you left."

"*You'd* barely talked to *me*. I practically stood on my head trying to get your attention." He moved her hand over his heart. "You were already pretty married to your job. Didn't ever look my way once."

She smiled. "I thought about you, Callahan."

He kissed her—but just briefly. "Get the dress. We're going. It's past time I got an 'I do' out of you."

"I can't get the dress. It's gone."

He looked at her. "Gone?"

"Disappeared. Just like that. If I hadn't hurried home, I would have been naked. I felt the dress changing while we were standing in the square."

"Naked wouldn't have been good," Dante said, "unless it's just for me." He looked worried. "Look in your closet."

She got up, looked inside the closet. "No gown."

"I'll check the attic storage."

Ana could tell Dante was worried by the way he shot up the stairs. She followed, still holding the one golden pump, wondering what was going on. In the attic, he flipped on the lights and flung open the storage door. "Nothing."

He turned to look at her. She swallowed nervously. "It just appeared in my closet tonight, Dante. With the shoes and the purse. I don't know why it disappeared."

"I know why," Dante said. "I've figured it out. It keeps disappearing because you have doubts. About you and me."

Chapter Seventeen

Ana shook her head, but Dante knew he'd hit the reason behind the gown's mysterious appearances and disappearances. "You're not sure. That's why you didn't see me before, when you tried the gown on originally."

"I don't know," Ana said. "I don't believe in superstitions and magic and fairy dust, Dante. I do think that if we were both certain that we belonged together, a relationship would have come to us more naturally. You're a bona fide bachelor, and I'm—"

"A bona fide bachelorette." Dante leaned against a post in the attic and sighed. "That's what this is about. It's not because of me, it's because you're worried about commitment from your end, doll face."

She wrinkled up her cute nose. "All Callahans have a reputation for being hard to tie down."

"True. But eventually, Callahans get caught."

"Catching you wasn't part of my plan," Ana said. "I don't believe in that, either."

"You're going to have to make up your mind, sweetheart. My son isn't going to like it when he asks you one day why you didn't marry Daddy, and you have to be honest and tell him it was because you had supercold feet when it came to commitment." He shook his head. "I don't think my son will like it at all. He's going to want a more traditional mother."

"You can't expect me to believe that you want to get married just because of a baby." She snapped her fingers. "Everything changes in a few hours, just because you find out you're going to be a father?" Ana stared at him. "You never proposed to me before."

"That's because," Dante said, "you've never given me a whole lot of reason to hope."

"I was trying to be professional. It seemed very unprofessional to be employed here and hit on my employer. While you weren't my direct employer, it wouldn't have been right to date you. River feels the same way about Tighe."

"She does?" Dante considered that. "No wonder he keeps bashing his brains out on a brick wall." He laughed. "Are you saying Tighe can keep trying to get River to go out with him, but it's not going to happen?" He couldn't help chuckling at his brother's plight. Once upon a time, he'd been there himself.

"Why are you laughing?" Ana asked.

"Because Tighe's making himself crazy for nothing." He turned serious. "But you're not employed here anymore, beautiful, so you just ran out of run as far as I'm concerned."

She looked at him. "I just don't know that you're ready to be married, Dante. You should have seen yourself on the stage tonight with your shirt off. The women were ready to rush the stage and carry you off."

"I was waiting for you to show up. By the way, you weren't in much of a hurry."

"Since I was stuck in the prop room, no, I couldn't rescue you as quickly as I wanted."

He smiled, unable to resist teasing her just a bit—

his little doll just did not want to admit how crazy for him she was. "I was annoyed with you for making me suffer in front of a hundred sexy women in mysterious masks for so long," he said with typical macho relish. "Still, you redeemed yourself when you ran in yelling, 'Five thousand dollars!' at the top of your lungs." He enjoyed letting her know that he was completely aware how much she dug him. "I forgave you on the— Wait, maybe we should talk more about why you were stuck in the prop room. What were you doing in there?"

Ana shot him a look of pure exasperation. It was such a darling expression he wanted to grab her up and kiss her until all the irritation melted from her face.

"Someone locked me in. So I couldn't rescue you as quickly as I'd promised—although if you asked me to rescue you again, I'm sure I'd refuse. Letting the she-wolves have you would be your just deserts."

He blinked. "Someone locked you in—and the first thing you did when you drew a free breath was sprint down the hall to shout out the winning bid for me. Ana St. John, you are lying like a rug if you say you don't want to marry me. No woman puts in a top bid unless she's serious about getting her man." He pulled her into his arms. "I know you're serious about me, sweetheart. Even if you haven't figured it out yet."

She wriggled away. "I said I'd rescue you, you oaf. And I was going to keep my word."

"I have to say," he said, regretting that he'd let her out of his arms so easily—she really was a stubborn thing, "that you could have heard a pin drop when Ash yelled out that the auction had to be cancelled due to the fact that I had a prior commitment. And that I was going to be a father, so my eligibility for the auction was suspect. I thought Fiona was going to fall over.

But then her eyes were twinkling, and I realized she was thrilled at the fact that one more of us was going to take the fall."

Ana sniffed. "Ash is a blabbermouth."

He reached out to draw her back to him. "I could have told you that. But I love her anyway. So who locked you in?"

"My guess is Sawyer, though I can't say for certain. She was determined to win you or your brother tonight. She didn't bother to bid on any of the other offerings. And if I ever have a chance to tell her just what I think of her little tricks, I will."

"You're jealous. I like it." He smiled broadly, unable to help himself.

She stiffened up like a cat confronted by a dog. "I am no such thing."

"You sure didn't want anybody else to win me." He kissed her, taking his time with her sweet lips. She unbent just a little, enough to let him know that even if she claimed she didn't believe in magic, there was plenty of it between them. "You won me. I suggest you seal the deal."

She left his arms. "If I say yes, it will change everything."

"Everything has already changed. I'd get on with tying me down, if I were you."

"Would you stop saying that? You're not helping." Ana glared at him. "No woman likes to feel that she's tying a man down. We like to be the catchee, not the catcher."

"If you want me to tie you down, beautiful, I'm more than happy to oblige, in more ways than one."

"This is exactly what I'm talking about. You're not serious about anything, Dante." She rewarded his teasing with a frown. "We're trying to talk about marriage, and you offer a sexual innuendo."

He smiled. "Yes, and my offer stands."

She sighed. "I think it's the pregnancy hormones that're muddling my thinking. I should be happy I won a Callahan, shouldn't I? That's what every woman there tonight wanted."

"Absolutely," Dante agreed, happy they both finally saw the situation the same way. "You won, fair and square. I say we hit Vegas and celebrate your success." He smiled, trying to coax her into losing her pensive expression. "I plan on celebrating by drinking champagne from your belly button. None for you, of course, because my son won't have his first alcoholic beverage until I buy it for him."

She sighed. "You will not drink champagne from my belly button."

"A man has to celebrate."

"They have glasses in Vegas, I feel certain." She shook her head. "Do you think I could get my old job back?"

He hesitated. "With Sloan and Kendall and the boys?"

She nodded.

"You can't be a bodyguard now, babe. You're pregnant. You're going to be a mom. You can't jeopardize our baby with a dangerous job."

"So that's it? I marry you, and I become a doll that sits on a shelf waiting for you to come home?"

"Uh-oh," Dante said, "this is the part of the conversation that's fraught with complexity. You're trying to sort out the future, when you should be thinking romance. Don't be practical right now, sugar lips. I'm trying to sweep you off your feet."

"What will happen, Dante?" she asked softly. "After we get married?"

"Well," he said slowly, realizing Ana's question was born of worry, which he very much understood, "you'll go to Hell's Colony with the other Callahans until the baby is born. Unless you wanted to go back to South Dakota."

She looked at him. "And if I want to stay here with you?"

"You of all people know it's not safe here."

"Because I'm not a bodyguard anymore. I'm a mom. I'd be a wife."

He didn't mistake the tension in her tone. "Things have changed."

She nodded. "Yes, they have."

Rats. She didn't look too thrilled. There wasn't anything he could do about the state of matters at the ranch. "You've been here long enough to know that everybody sacrifices. At least until things are fixed."

"It may never be fixed," Ana said. "Wolf may never be stopped. The cartel may never give up. I'll never be a bodyguard again."

"You'll be a mother," Dante said softly, "and that's what you wanted."

She brightened. "Yes. Exactly. But I want to be a mother who's respected for the skills she has."

"You want to stay here at the ranch, and safeguard your child."

"I can take care of myself, and my child," Ana pointed out. "I don't want to be put in a bow-wrapped box just because I've become a mother."

"I get it," Dante said, "but it will make me crazy."

"You're already crazy. Will something change?"

"No," he said carefully, "but all the other mothers left."

"You may have to compromise," Ana said.

"I suppose we could hire a bodyguard like Kendall did," Dante began, but Ana shook her head.

"Your hearing is going, Callahan. I can take care of my own child. I don't want to be sent away. I want to be respected for what I do. I'm a damn good bodyguard."

"I know. You saved me a time or two." He scratched his head. "You're asking me to go against my male chauvinistic grain. You're asking a leopard to change its spots. You're—"

"It's okay," Ana said. "You'd survive the slight knock to your ego."

"I don't know if I would. It's pretty much my stock in trade."

Ana went down the stairs. He followed her, wondering if maybe she was softening her stance just a bit. Maybe he finally had her convinced to marry him. He could pretend that he was allowing her to stay at the ranch, and then send her off to Hell's Colony on some pretext. Or he could station a few separate guards on her without mentioning it. Compromise was something he could live with—on his terms.

"So, are we going?" he asked Ana as she went out the door. "To Vegas? Or someplace that does quickies? I really think we should teach our child the value of timeliness and promptitude."

Ana turned, gave him a long look. "Am I staying here at the ranch? With you? Instead of you sending me off?"

He hedged. "You know, if I were still in the military and I was deployed again, I'd be leaving and that would just be that. Why don't we just consider you leaving the ranch your deployment?"

She gave him a look of disgust. "Because I'm fine. I want to be a real wife, not a marriage of convenience wife, just because you wanted to win the ranch land."

"That's dumb," he said, "there is no ranch land. There is no race for it. I want you to be my wife because you're having my baby, and mostly because you make me crazy. Good crazy."

"You were crazy, Dante," Ana said, "long before I ever came along. And there's something I think you're overlooking. Someone went to Hell's Colony on Halloween and took out the sniper, then you and I were kidnapped. Ash and Xav were tied up and left in the canyon by someone who intended to go back and get them. Then I got shoved into a prop room at the masquerade ball."

He tried to see her point, had to admit that once again, she was thinking more strategically than he was. "Someone has a thing for bondage and revenge?"

She sighed. "Fiona has floated a fairy tale for you Callahans. She says Storm Cash bought the land, but somehow, Rancho Diablo is still under siege from your uncle Wolf's mercenaries. Storm's niece Sawyer pushes me into a closet to put a winning bid on you."

"She bid for Tighe, too. And won."

"Exactly. The goal was to get one of you alone with her."

"Ah, a sexy spy thing," he said. "Maybe you're just a tiny bit jealous?"

"What I am trying to tell you is that Storm is setting you guys up. Fiona actually bought the land, but Storm wanted it. Wolf asked Storm to buy the land, told him that he'd quit trespassing on his land if he did, and that he'd use the land north of the canyons to trespass instead. But if you look through the county records, Fiona's and Running Bear's names are on the deed for that land. Wolf's annoyed that Fiona got the property—bought it right out from under him, when he thought the old farmer was going to do a deal with Storm. The whole thing with us being kidnapped, and Xav and Ash getting attacked, is because Wolf is desperately trying to make Fiona give up the land. That's why Sawyer winning Tighe tonight is troubling. Someone has to keep an eye on Fiona, and Kendall and the boys. No one can do it better than me and River."

He stared at Ana, thunderstruck. "Where are you getting all this?"

"It's my job as a bodyguard to be observant."

"Yeah, but you—you're touting some pretty incredible stuff. Why wouldn't Fiona keep dangling the ranch land in front of us if she owns it?"

"Because she and Running Bear are planning to split the ranch up, bring your Callahan cousins home from Hell's Colony, start a new arm of the Callahan operation. Fiona says it's time to bring the family home from Hell's Colony, Texas." She stared at Dante. "They don't want you all to marry in hopes for land, just in case she has to split it up."

He sank onto a kitchen bar stool, staring at Ana. "How do you know all this?"

"If I tell you, you have to accept that I belong here. That I'm good at what I do, and that you and I should work together, as a team. Not you sending the little woman off to be safe. I really can't stand it when you act like a he-man," Ana said, and he thought it was cute when she was a little huffy. "You say you'll compromise, but when you say that, you really mean as long as it's all on your terms."

"Well," he said, not really wanting to admit she'd pegged him dead center, "I could go along with the teamwork notion. I guess. Reluctantly. If you marry me."

"Not reluctantly. Enthusiastically. As in, you have my back and I have yours. No sneaking around me, trying to protect me."

"You *are* carrying my child," he pointed out, suppressing his queasiness at the thought of Wolf kidnapping his darling, opinionated bodyguard–baby mama.

"I'm carrying our child," Ana said, "and he's happy being here with his father."

Dante considered that. "You really mean that, don't you?"

"Of course I do." She smiled. "Jonathan Dante has a perfectly good father he needs to get to know as soon as possible."

Dante sighed. "You win. I'm a sucker for sweet talk. Now tell me how you know everything you're surmising."

"I had a chat with Sawyer."

He stared. "When?"

"After she won Tighe. My guess is Sawyer's a double agent, but don't tell your brother. I want to see where this goes."

"She admitted she was a double agent?" Dante guided Ana outside and put her in the jeep.

"No. But she wouldn't have worked so hard to get with a Callahan if she wasn't."

"Ouch," Dante said, "watch the ego, please."

"Wolf is smart to utilize her. But she's not a mercenary. Sawyer doesn't know about intrigue. She thinks she's just doing what her uncle has asked her to do, which is to get him information," Ana told him. "That's why she struck up a conversation with me. She didn't know I was from Rancho Diablo, I was wearing a mask." Ana shrugged. "She said he is always very curious about the Callahans. Of course she's going to find out what she can and tell him. Wouldn't you do that for your aunt?" She looked at him curiously. "Where are we going?"

"To Las Vegas," Dante said. "You said if I agreed, you'd marry me."

"I didn't mean in blue jeans!"

"Uh-uh. I'm not giving you time to crawfish on me. If I tell you we can wait until you find a wedding gown, you'll find a new excuse to stay just out of my reach." On this point, Dante was certain. "I know this because magic wedding dresses have a tendency to disappear around you. What chance does a garden variety, unenchanted off-the-rack dress have with your track record with wedding gowns?" He smiled to show her he was teasing—even though he kind of wasn't. "Besides, if we get too close to the holidays, Elvis might take a ride with Santa Claus. I'm not risking the holiday schedule for drive-through weddings." He caught her hand in his. "I think this teamwork thing will work out just fine."

"Good," Ana said, "because I've been doing a lot of thinking, ever since I found out I was having a baby. I know how I'm going to stay here and still do bodyguard work."

His blood went a little chilly. Okay, maybe the teamwork thing wasn't going to be so awesome. This was probably the part where he was supposed to say, "Great! Tell me all about it!"

"That's…great, babe. You mean, like when Jon Dante's all grown up, right?"

"No," Ana said, "I've decided to open a bodyguard school at Rancho Diabo for ladies only. And just so you know, Running Bear and Fiona wholeheartedly approve."

Chapter Eighteen

Dante swallowed hard, tried not to let worry show on his face. "School for bodyguards?"

"That's right. Women only." Ana nodded. "I'm really excited about it. River and I will plan to run the school together. I didn't want to tell you until I knew you'd be okay with me staying in Diablo."

Dante drove the jeep down the road. "That's great. I mean it."

"That's why you're gripping the steering wheel so hard your knuckles are locked." Ana put a hand on his arm. "Your blood pressure's shooting out your head."

"I'll get used to it," Dante said, meaning it. "Just go slowly with me, okay? It's not easy to get over male chauvinism when you've reveled in it all your life."

She smiled. "I'm not starting the school until Jon Dante starts kindergarten."

"Oh," he said, breathing a sigh of relief. "Whatever you think is best." He felt very magnanimous as he said it.

"I've waited too long to be a mother to do anything but spend every second with Jon Dante."

He grinned. "That sounds great." He slowed down,

realizing he was, indeed, clenching the steering wheel. "So we're getting married tonight?"

"I don't want a quickie wedding. We'd regret it later. As much as I know you love being Mr. Action, you're also very deliberate and thoughtful. Considering marriage requires sincere thought, don't you think?"

He swallowed. "I guess I'll turn this can around then. You sure you won't drag me to the altar tonight?"

"You get to stay wild and crazy a little while longer."

He looked over at her, thinking the last thing he wanted to be was wild and crazy. "I'm crazy for you. How long are you going to let me roam the range?"

"Seven days is probably long enough for you to decide you don't want to give up rodeo and walking on the wild side."

His heart sank. "It will be the longest seven days of my life. We could do a little pre-wedding tonight, just a warm-up act, and then do it again in a week," he said. "Life is short. All the Callahan brides get married twice."

"I look forward to being the first to say 'I do' only once," Ana said. "A Christmas wedding will be beautiful."

"I was never good at waiting," Dante said, worrying. "I'm a pull-the-trigger kind of guy. You did just offer five thousand dollars for me. Even though the auction was canceled, I think you should go ahead and have me."

"I need some time," Ana said, and his heart nearly stopped.

"Time? That sounds inconclusive."

"Do you ever wonder why the magic wedding dress disappeared again?"

He shook his head. "No, I don't. If I see that trouble-some rag again, I'm going to—"

"Shh!" She glanced at him. "Did you hear something?"

"Sounded like someone honking." He glanced over his shoulder. "Someone's following us, but they don't have their lights on."

She turned around to peek. "They don't want us to see them."

"Here's our options," Dante said, "we drive to Sheriff Cartwright's office and see if our friends back there care to continue this game so close to the jail."

"Like that idea," Ana said, "and the other option?"

"There may still be revelers in the square," Dante pointed out.

"You're right." Ana glanced over her shoulder again. "We don't want to endanger anyone. Slow down and see if they pass. Could be that it's your brothers and they forgot to turn on their lights. Or they're playing a Callahan practical joke."

A tap on their bumper sent the truck flying forward about a foot. "We can rule out my brothers," Dante said. "How do you feel about speed instead of slowing down?"

"Suddenly I'm quite interested in seeing your driving skills."

"Good." He sped up a fraction, keeping one eye on the road conditions and one on the rearview mirror. "Do you prefer a handgun or a rifle? The rifle's on the rack, the .38's in the glove box. Just in case."

"Both are fine, but we'll start off with the handgun if needed." She dug it out and loaded it. "I assume you're heading to Sheriff Cartwright's instead of the ranch?"

"Give him a call, would you, gorgeous? Let him know we're coming and could use a welcoming committee?"

She dialed her cell phone, made the request, hung up. "Good news for you, the partygoers are nowhere near the jail. Everybody is still partying near the theater. Apparently, your brothers are leading karaoke Christmas carols."

"That just sounds unfortunate from a family reputation point of view."

"But the sheriff says there's so much hot cocoa and hot cider flowing that the square may not be cleared until dawn."

"Fiona and her parties." He went slowly around the bend, headed to town. "The lifeblood of Diablo. They still back there?"

"Yes. Which surprises me because you're driving like a turtle. You think they'd get bored and go throw snowballs or something."

"You just keep your seat belt on good and your head down. Tell my son Daddy's got this."

Ana sighed. "Mommy and Daddy have this handled. Together."

"That's what I meant to say. You just say everything better than I do. Duly noted?"

"Sure. Sheriff Cartwright said to pull around behind the jail. He's got a welcome party waiting back there for our friends."

"We are so friendly in this town." He pulled into the parking lot, happy when they were followed. The sheriff's men suddenly jumped out from their hidden posts, swarming the car, dragging someone out.

"Who is it?" Ana asked Dante.

"I don't know him. If I ask you to stay back while

I go talk to him, will you take that to mean I'm not an advocate of our teamwork plan?"

"You gave me a gun to shoot him, but you don't want me to talk to him?"

"Silly me. Darn those protective urges. Come on."

They walked together to the car and the perp, who was handcuffed and being searched, stared them down.

"Did you want to talk to me, buddy?" Dante asked.

"Just want to make sure you know we're around," he replied, and Ana gasped.

"I know who you are! You're one of the men who tied up Ash and Xav."

Dante looked at her. "How do you know?"

"Ash mentioned a facial scar. And Falcon's wife, Taylor, said he was one of the men who kidnapped her and held her up north for months."

"You're lucky," the bandit told her, "we nearly got you."

"What's the point?" she asked him. "Who are you?"

"Name's Rhine, not that it will do you any good to know." He grinned at her, and it was ugly. "Eventually, we'll get one of you. If not you, your bodyguard buddy who works with you. You don't really think we wouldn't use a woman to get what we want, do you? In the end, Wolf will win."

"That's enough," Sheriff Cartwright said. "Threatening someone will get you in trouble, son. Read him his rights, we'll figure out plenty more charges later," he told a deputy, and they took their prisoner away.

"Best you stay close to home, Ana," Sheriff Cartwright said. "Let Dante and the boys look after you. Dante, you swing by and make a statement after you take Ana home."

"Will do." Dante turned to lead her to the truck. Ana practically puffed up like a rooster on him.

"I'm not going back to the ranch to be treated like a helpless princess," Ana said.

"Yeah, you are." Dante took her arm and led her away. "You're pregnant, and you need rest. Heck, I need rest, and I'm not carrying a child. This has been a night I'll never forget."

She went with him, albeit reluctantly. "I can handle this situation, Dante. You can't change just because tonight you learned I'm expecting a baby."

"I did change," Dante said, "although I admit I didn't do it consciously. All I know is that you and River are the only females on the ranch—"

"What about Fiona and Ashlyn? And Kendall?"

"Yes, but…"

"But they can take care of themselves," Ana said, her tone annoyed.

"It's different. Come on, hot baby."

She got in the truck. "I am not a hot baby." She glared at him as he started the truck. "You're being pigheaded."

"Probably just best to deal with it," he said, then leaned over to kiss her. She tasted good, smelled good—it was all he could not to just ride off into the proverbial sunset with her. "Last chance to take me to Vegas, gorgeous. Otherwise, I'm dropping you off with whoever's staggered back to the ranch from the party."

"Fine."

His brows shot up. "Fine what?"

"Let's hit Vegas."

"Are you serious?" He couldn't believe she'd change her mind. There was a trap here he was about to step into, and Dante waited for it. Was it too good to be true?

"Very serious."

"Why?" He started the engine. If his lady was game, he was going to drive to the airport with all due haste.

"Because you're a good man. Because I've loved you for a long time. And because I understand that you're trying to protect me. Being your wife isn't going to change my independence."

He smiled. "I love your independence. Nobody knows better than me that I can be a bit overbearing at times. I want you to be happy. I want to make you happy. Ignore me when I get too overbearing."

"Ignore me when I'm too worried about my independence. It's precious to me, but I want to be a good wife and mother, too."

"So we're off?"

A rapping on the window stopped their conversation. Dante slid it down. "Hi, Aunt Fiona."

She peered through at Ana, her little face worried. "Sheriff Cartwright says someone chased you tonight."

"We're fine, Fiona. Don't worry," Ana said.

"The family should handle their own business." She glanced at Dante. "You're going to be a father, you know, and Ana's no longer employed by Rancho Diablo. She shouldn't be involved in these things. Ana, come with me, dear. I'm going to get you a nice cup of hot cider. It will calm everybody's nerves."

She went around to Ana's door, opening it, shooing her out.

"Aunt Fiona," Dante said, "we were actually about to—"

"It's all right," Ana said quickly. "I'm going with your aunt."

His jaw dropped. "Hold on a red-hot second!" He

hopped out of the truck. "You were going to Vegas with me!"

"Vegas?" Fiona shook her head. "The airport is closed due to inclement weather. Don't you listen to weather reports on your radio?"

"Not when I'm being chased by nefarious types," Dante muttered, his dreams going up in smoke. "Are you absolutely certain?"

"Certain as I always am," Fiona said cheerfully, sounding too pleased especially for someone who loved weddings as much as she did. "Give up the whole notion, is my advice."

She led Ana off with her, leaving Dante to park his truck and stew. He loped after his aunt and his almost-bride, the snow slushing around his boots as he hurried. "Ladies, throw a guy a bone here."

Ana smiled over his aunt's head. "Maybe it's for the best. Give us a chance to think things over."

"Thinking is not good," Dante said. "I much prefer not thinking when possible. I'm a man of action, what can I say?"

"Surprise, surprise," Fiona said. "Do you have a ring for your bride? An indication of your affections? A plan for a honeymoon? Anything romantic?"

Ana raised a brow at him as he considered his aunt's question. "No," he admitted, "but rolling with the flow is kind of my thing."

"Well, the snow should be gone by Christmas. Then you could get married a few days after that, when things slow down just a bit. Give you time to get your act together, nephew. Come on, Ana, let's close this party down."

Dante watched his favorite women walk off, somewhat bemused. It was true he wasn't the prince sweeping the princess off her feet. He didn't have a ring, really had no plan except to get her to the altar.

No wonder Ana wasn't jumping for joy.

But she had agreed to marry him. Sort of. He'd caught her in a spontaneous moment.

Rhine had said Wolf's plan was eventually to pick off one of the women, knowing very well that the women of Rancho Diablo were the heart and soul of the Callahans' lives. Dante didn't figure any of his brothers would be the men they were without the women they'd chosen. Sloan and Falcon were certainly better men now with wives and families. "Look at Galen and Jace and Tighe, dangling in the wind," he murmured. "They need good women."

He himself would be a better man with Ana, and well did he know it. "Help, help!" he yelled.

Ana and Fiona turned around, stared at him curiously.

"Nephew, whatever has gotten into your pumpkin head?" Fiona demanded.

"Help!" he said more urgently, waving his arms for dramatic effect.

"He's a retired SEAL," Fiona told Ana. "I promise he is neither helpless nor as odd as he appears at this moment, wailing in the center of the square."

Ana walked over, stood in front of him. "Dante, you're yelling, in case you didn't realize it."

"Oh, I know," he said. "I need help badly. I didn't realize it until just this second, but I do." He could feel himself exuding earnestness, and he pressed his point. "Here's the deal. You're a bodyguard, right? I'm a guy who needs saving from myself. I want you to protect me. Rescue me. Otherwise I'm going to end up like

Galen and Jace and Tighe, and that's just not a happy ending."

She smiled. "It's not a bad ending. They're nice guys."

"Yeah, but they don't have what I've got." He stared at her, knowing every word was true. "You're worried marrying me will mean your independence is gone. But I don't think you realize how much I depend on you to be my better half."

"Dante, that's sweet. I think you're ladling it on a bit thick, but—"

He pulled her to him, kissed her gently. "I can't ladle this on thick enough. Fiona's right, I have left off the romance, the touches that count." He took a deep breath. "Sometimes I am spontaneous. But something that's never changed is how much I love you. I adored you from afar before I ever knew you'd give me half a minute of a day, Ana. The truth is, I'm thrilled to be a father, but I wanted you no matter what. You're not a means to an end to me, you are the reason I know I can be a better man. Be my bodyguard, babe. I need saving like nothing you can imagine."

Tears jumped into Ana's eyes. "You know you didn't have to say any of this. I'd already agreed to marry you."

He swept her into his arms, carried her back to his truck. "Sorry, Aunt Fiona," he called over his shoulder, "we've got our own party to attend."

"That's fine," Fiona said. "It's nice to see you figured out which of you is the true grand prize!"

"She's so good for my ego," Dante told Ana, and Ana laughed, laying her head against his shoulder. "I love you," he said, and Ana kissed him, and Dante knew he was the luckiest man on the earth. He helped her into his truck, loving it when she wrapped her arms around him for another kiss before sliding back in the seat.

"I feel like a prince taking his princess off into the sunset," Dante said. He stared at the twinkling thing on the dash, picked it up carefully. "Did you know you left your shoe in my truck?"

Ana shook her head. "I didn't leave that here."

Dante grinned. "Guess you know what this means?"

"I have a shoe that needs a mate?"

He laughed. "No. It means I really have found my princess. The magic slipper fit only one special lady, and I do believe in fairy tales." He gave her his most devilish wink. "What do you say we head back to the ranch and let me slip it on you, in case you have any doubts that you're the only one for me?"

"Is that what you're really planning to do once we get back to the ranch?" Ana asked. "Put my shoes on?"

"No," Dante said, kissing her, this time taking his time, "I plan on showing you that my heart belongs only to you."

"Now that's a happy ending," Ana said, "get this coach moving, cowboy."

The golden pump twinkled as if it was glittered with fairy dust, and as they drove home together, Dante heard thunder in the distance, wild and free, rolling across the Diablo skies. And if it wasn't just his heart jumping for happiness but the sound of the Diablo mustangs, dancing the song of spirits that had always guided him, who was to know the difference?

"I love you so much," Ana whispered, and Dante smiled.

He'd found his home at last.

Epilogue

Dante watched as Ana walked down the aisle on a sunlit day in December. Ashlyn was her maid of honor, appropriate because those two were like-minded adventurers, sisters in independent spirit. Tighe served as his best man, and Dante had never been happier to have his twin at his side. Rancho Diablo was filled with friends and family enjoying the day. Tomorrow was Christmas Eve and the holiday madness would begin, but today was for celebrating the real gifts in his life—the Christmas miracles he still could hardly believe were his.

Ana reached his side, and Dante grinned hugely. "Babe, you're beautiful. White looks great on you. The red was sexy, but white is a knockout."

Ana smiled. "It's the most gorgeous wedding dress I've ever seen. It's not too traditional for you?"

"Nope. I'm all about tradition, as everyone knows. Mr. Traditional is my nickname. And today, I'm the luckiest traditional guy on the planet."

"You won't get an argument from me." Ana's eyes twinkled.

"So," he said on a whisper, "did you see me when you put on the magic wedding gown?"

"Not exactly."

He blinked. "I'm glad you didn't let that freak you out. Fiona's fairy tales get a little out of hand at times."

"Yet you're the first to admit that your aunt is usually right." Dante could tell his bride was having a bit of fun at his expense, which was all right by him. "Dante, I saw *us*."

He felt better immediately. "That sounds like it was worth apologizing to the dress for, then."

"You apologized to my wedding gown?" Ana looked as though she was trying not to laugh, but Dante didn't care.

"I most certainly apologized to the magic. No way was I going to have my bride in a vanishing gown!" Dante pondered that for a moment. "Although it can vanish all it wants as soon as I have you behind a locked door." He kissed her, not waiting for the deacon to tell him he could, and it felt pretty magical just feeling her lips against his. He couldn't wait to be a husband to the only woman who could have made him want to be married so badly that he counted the seconds until the moment she said "I do."

"I saw you and me, and our baby," Ana said. "We were happy. We were a family."

His heart swelled with joy. "I can't wait until July. You're going to be an amazing mother."

Ana smiled, practically glowing. Heck, she was glowing, like an angel. Dante wasn't really surprised. He'd always known his girl was heavenly.

"Thank you for saying that, Dante. It means everything to me."

He winked. "Of course, I knew that getting you pregnant was the only way to get you to the altar," he said softly, for her ears alone. "Lucky for me, you were so eager to marry me. I barely looked at you, and boom! I'm at the altar. I expect lots of praise from you over the years, beautiful."

"I wonder if Jon Dante will get his father's ego?" Ana teased.

"I just hope he gets my smarts. I'm marrying the woman of my dreams. I love you, Ana, with all my heart and soul. I cover those emotions sometimes because it's hard to put my feelings into words. But you're my dream come true, babe. My everything. Marrying you is the kind of miracle a man spends hours of his life praying for."

Tears jumped into Ana's eyes. "Dante, that's sweet. You make me run my mascara and you're going to have a creepy-looking bride in the pictures. What will our son say when he looks at our wedding photos?"

"Probably that I was smart to tie you down and brand you Callahan." Dante was extremely pleased with himself as he drew a smile from his bodyguard bride. "Deacon, start the ceremony if you will. I have a family to marry."

She laughed. "I think I'm the one marrying the family."

"True. Brave woman."

"I'm a Callahan," Ana said. "I'm going to be Mrs. Dante Callahan." She glanced down at the lovely engagement ring he'd picked out for her, with Ash's help. His sister had steered him to buy a diamond the size of a dime—Ash said she appreciated the irony after Tighe had thrown all of his twin's money into Tighe's barrel at the Christmas masquerade ball. Ana smiled. "I always wondered what it would feel like to be a Callahan, and now I know."

"So, how does it feel?" Dante asked.

"So magical I can't even describe it," Ana said, and he could tell she meant ever word. "The best thing I ever did was fall head over heels in love with you."

And that was the reward, wasn't it? The happy ending for all the years he'd thought he'd never settle down, his long search for what he was missing, now given to him by his amazing bride. Dante heard the thunder of the mystical Diablos running in the canyons, saw Running Bear sitting astride a Diablo in the distance, and heartfelt joy swept his soul. He had everything he needed now, and it was better than a fairy tale.

It was magic.

* * * * *

Tighe is the next Callahan to be caught!
Watch for CALLAHAN COWBOY TRIPLETS,
coming in September 2013,
only from Harlequin American Romance!

#1461 THE LONG, HOT TEXAS SUMMER
McCabe Homecoming
Cathy Gillen Thacker

Businessman Justin McCabe starts a ranch for troubled boys, but it turns out former delinquent Amanda Johnson is better at dealing with the teens than he is, and she is offered Justin's job!

#1462 HIS FOREVER VALENTINE
Forever, Texas
Marie Ferrarella

For Rafe Rodriguez, saving a beautiful city slicker from a charging bull is well worth the danger. Now can he convince her to give him, and Texas, a chance?

#1463 HER SECRET, HIS BABY
The Colorado Cades
Tanya Michaels

Rancher Garrett Frost is surprised when he runs into sexy Arden Cade again six months after their one incredible night together. But he's *really* surprised to learn he's going to be a daddy!

#1464 HOME TO THE COWBOY
Amanda Renee

Tess Dalton and Cole Langtry just can't get over their falling-out the night Cole meant to propose. Can Ever, an orphaned four-year-old, be the glue that holds them together for good?

SPECIAL EXCERPT FROM

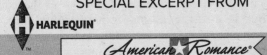

HARLEQUIN®

American ★ Romance®

THE LONG, HOT TEXAS SUMMER
by Cathy Gillen Thacker

The second book in the McCABE HOMECOMING *series.*

Welcome back to Laramie County, Texas, where things are heating up between Justin McCabe and his new carpenter!

There were times for doing-it-yourself and times for not, Justin McCabe thought grimly, surveying the damage he had just inadvertently inflicted on a brand-new utility cabinet.

It was possible, of course, this could be fixed, without buying a whole new cabinet. If he knew what he was doing. Which he did not—a fact the five beloved ranch mutts, sitting quietly, cautiously watching his every move, seemed to realize, too.

A motor sounded in the lane.

Hoping it was the carpenter who was supposed to be there that morning, Justin walked to the door of Bunkhouse #1, just as a fancy red extended-cab Silverado pickup truck pulled up in front of the lodge. It had an equally elaborate travel trailer attached to the back. A lone woman was at the wheel.

"Great." Justin sighed as all the dogs darted out of the open door of the partially finished bunkhouse and raced, barking their heads off, toward her.

The lost tourist eased the window down and stuck her head out into the sweltering Texas heat. A straw hat with a sassily rolled brim perched on her head. Sunglasses shaded her eyes. But there was no disguising her beautiful face. With her sexy shoulders and incredibly buff bare arms, the interloper was, without a doubt, the most staggeringly beautiful female Justin had ever seen.

She smiled at the dogs. "Hey, poochies," she greeted them softly and melodically.

As entranced as he was, they simply sat down and stared.

She opened her door and stepped out. All six feet of her.

A double layer of red-and-white tank tops showcased her nice, full breasts and slender waist. A short denim skirt clung to her hips and showcased a pair of really fine legs. Her equally sexy feet were encased in a pair of red flip flops.

She took off her hat and shook out a mane of butterscotch hair that fell in soft waves past her shoulders. She turned and tossed the hat on the seat behind her, then reached down to pet his five rescue dogs in turn. The pack was thoroughly besotted.

Justin completely understood.

If there was such a thing as love at first sight—which he knew there wasn't—he'd be a goner.

THE LONG, HOT TEXAS SUMMER
by Cathy Gillen Thacker.
Available August 6, 2013,
from Harlequin® American Romance®.
And watch for two more books in the series this summer!

SADDLE UP AND READ 'EM!

Looking for another great Western read? Check out these August reads from the HOME & FAMILY category!

THE LONG, HOT TEXAS SUMMER by Cathy Gillen Thacker
McCabe Homecoming
Harlequin American Romance

HOME TO THE COWBOY by Amanda Renee
Harlequin American Romance

HIS FOREVER VALENTINE by Marie Ferrarella
Forever, Texas
Harlequin American Romance

THE MAVERICK'S SUMMER LOVE by Christyne Butler
Montana Mavericks
Harlequin Special Edition

*Look for these great Western reads AND MORE
available wherever books are sold or visit*
www.Harlequin.com/Westerns